The Village Tradesman

Kyuka Lilymjok

ISBN 978-978-928-528-0

Published by:
Free Pen Publishers
10 Lachlan Close, Maitama, Abuja

Contents

To my wife Maria and my children: Justice, Sunfair and Fairprincess.

Sleep, the vulture of the night
Could not peck his flesh
Because he was in the bush
Looking for a stone axe
To break the coffin of poverty

Chapter One

A Man and his Trade

Sunday, May 4th

For twenty-seven years now, Mallam Nuhu has been a hawker of women ornaments such as earrings, bangles, necklaces, eyebrow cosmetics and other assorted women adornments. The articles of his trade were cheap wares that held no appeal to urban women, particularly those of them with means. But in the villages, they were sought after by rural women whose tastes in such articles were largely commonplace. Besides women trinkets, Mallam Nuhu also hawked garlic which is a vaccine against pneumonia and other cold related ailments. Ginger and other porridge seasoning ingredients such as *kajiji, masoro, kaminfari, fasakwari, kimba and kulla,* were other articles of his trade.

From village to village, he moved in and out of season hawking his wares to rural patronage with means. Over the years, he has gone through villages like Nakwana, Buka Takwas, Kahugo, Kurmin Kuza, Jemage, Malmala, Kyalli, Shuruba, Yaddakunni, Jita, Gadamari, Wakiluwa, Macibi, Dondoni, Auchan, Baucha, Landa, Honaka, Talabiya, and a host of other villages round and about the Darakuwa Plateau many times than any mind in these villages could recall. In these villages, he was known by villagers that patronised his trade as *dankoli*. But to an uninvolved passer-by, he was the village tradesman. The children knew him. They played with him and he played with them. Sometimes, he made gifts of *kulikuli*, *bazarkwela* and *alewa* to them. Like patronisers of his trade, they called him dankoli. Often, their shouts of '*dankoli* has come!' was the siren that announced his arrival in a village.

Mallam Nuhu was a simple ordinary man. The sort of man that commands no second look. Of slight frame, tall and wary in disposition, the only remarkable aspect of the man was his long, white cap that marked him out as a chef out of favour with his vocation. On all occasions, the cap was to be seen before the man. That was when he moved without the wares of his trade. But when he walked with the articles of his trade in his tray, the cap would suffer an eclipse. Then the tray containing the articles of his trade would be delicately balanced on his head while his hands swung back and forth in locomotive aid to his legs. On the few occasions he rode any of his two rickety bicycles with the tray containing his articles, he was a spectacle to behold. On such occasions, his neck took a rigid poise that concentrated the centre of gravity of the tray on the nucleus of his skull. Whenever the neck enjoyed a sway, his head and the tray swayed along before the neck would snap them to attention, once more. Never was it seen or heard that the tray left his head to spill its contents on the ground on account of a variance in the rhythm of his movement.

In the Darakuwa Plateau he traded, very few villagers knew where Mallam Nuhu came from – his hometown. Some of them suspected he did not know where he came from either. To these villagers, he belonged to those rare species of humans that bear no biological relationship to anyone. Thus seen, his articles of trade stood incarnated as his only relations. The man and his trade then wove into each other like a matting nest. The anonymity of his person in a curious way accentuated the value of his wares in the eyes of some of the villagers.

Years over years, Mallam Nuhu had traversed rivers, hills and forests to take his wares to rural areas of the Darakuwa Plateau. Like a bitten missionary, his commitment to taking his wares to the remotest hamlet was legendary. Unlike a missionary, however, Mallam Nuhu has no eternal life. Earthly fortune was the crown of glory his faraway look fixed. He traded on with this crown before him, leading him by day like a pillar of cloud, and by night like a pillar of fire to every hamlet round and afar the Plateau.

This particular Sunday morning, he was in high spirit as he climbed his bicycle in preparation to depart for Nakwana village situated in the western part of the Darakuwa Plateau. The tray containing his wares was on his head unsupported by a hand; his right foot was on the right pedal while the left foot was on the ground. With a nudging movement, he pressed the right foot against the right pedal and the bicycle began to move. His left foot on the ground moved along to ride on the left pedal.

The high spirit apparent about him, seemingly, was not shared by his bicycle, which had an abject and melancholic appearance about it. Each push of the pedal by either foot, but perhaps more by the left foot, appeared by the creaking sounds from the old bicycle, to inflict more pain on the bicycle than the one before it. It was like the bicycle was mourning. If it was mourning, it was in for a long mourning as Mallam Nuhu was set to ride it far that day. As he pedalled on, the bicycle which had seen more Sundays than Mallam Nuhu was disposed upon such consideration to be gentler with its pedals went on sniffing here and wailing there depending on the agony of the trip. The vagabond that would eat no man's dust rattled from plains to highlands through dense forests leaving behind it a nimbus of dust for its guard of honour, the grasses and wayside shrubs, to eat.

This year, the rains were late in coming. The first rain in the Darakuwa Plateau and its neighbourhood usually came sometime in the month of March. But it was not too unusual for it to come at the end of February. This year, for weeks long after the first rain was expected, the sun shone with a blazing intensity that spelt terror on earth. Each day, the sun rose a little earlier than usual and stayed up in the sky a little longer than before. Farmers were becoming very anxious.

Today was a bright, sunny day that promised a very hot afternoon. The sun rising from the east carried a drum of heat with it, which it was beating at regular intervals to a blazing pitch as it rose higher into the sky. From where he set out, it normally took him a whole day on his bicycle to reach Binjiri, which was not very far from Nakwana. Usually, he rode the bicycle up to Binjiri where he bought more articles of his trade. He would then pass the night in Binjiri, and the following morning, proceed to Nakwana on foot, leaving his bicycle in the house of Nabegu his trusted friend in Binjiri. The other bicycle, not any newer than the one he was riding now, he rode mostly between the villages of Landa, Baucha and Buka Takwas. For this reason, it was to be found in any of these villages whenever he was not using it.

The road between Binjiri and Nakwana was a thorny, hilly road that most times Mallam Nuhu attempted riding his bicycle through, he ended up with a punctured tyre. Then, he had to push the bicycle along with his wares up and down the many hilly and sloppy points of the road. He did not like this. He would rather carry his wares on his head and be sure of not pushing a bicycle than risk the road with a bicycle only to end up being *rode* by the bicycle as he would say when he had to push a punctured bicycle.

Chapter Two

Ant Lessons

Mallam Nuhu had learned his lessons of industry from the ants of his savannah country. Born in Northern Nigeria, he had only Koranic education in those days western education was taking its first roots in Northern Nigeria. As a child in the country, he took an unusual interest in anthills. He was always fascinated whenever he passed by ants in the process of constructing an anthill called *Jiba* in Hausa language. He would stop walking and regard closely the procession of industry at the hill construction site. Later, it became his regular appointment to visit an anthill in construction every evening. He would tear off some leaves from shrubs about the anthill in construction to sit and watch the intriguing proceedings of the ants at labour. While some ants dived down the womb of the earth to bring bits of moist soil for the construction, some ferried in bits of grasses and other ants' food items into the hill under construction. For once the anthill was constructed, access by the ants to food outside was limited. He would peep inside the hill under construction trying to integrate himself into the process. The crevices, partitions and abysses of the hill excited his architectural fancy. 'How safer humans and their property would have been if they were masters of the architectural skills of the ants,' he would think.

Because Mallam Nuhu cherished the ants as their hills, he was loathed to destroy an anthill for the sake of engaging the ants in a labour he loved watching. Therefore, unless he happened upon an anthill in the process of construction, it was not for him to smash a completed anthill to meet his sport. Thus, some evenings found him combing large tracks of bushland trying to find an anthill in the process of construction. However, as farmers and other children were in the process of smashing anthills, he was rarely in want of anthills in the process of construction to engage his pastime.

One evening, in the dry season, he was returning from the forest with his father when he sighted an anthill under construction beside the path.

'Baba, that anthill; now that it is dry season, where do the ants building the hill get water for their building?' he asked his father, pointing at the anthill under construction.

'The ants are water reservoirs themselves,' his father answered.

'Baba, I don't understand.'

'I mean their bellies are water reservoirs,' the father said. 'So, all they need do to get water for their present business is to vomit some of the water from their reservoirs and the business behind us will be under way.'

'I was thinking of some well, underground stream or a …'

'Perhaps those as well.'

'But Baba, what if the water in their reservoirs dries up before the rainy season and the construction is yet to be completed, what happens?'

'That should be their headache, I suppose. But go back there tomorrow and see if that hill is not completed.'

'Another thing Baba; how do ants survive drowning in the rainy season when the earth becomes saturated with water?'

'My son, since you take more than a passing interest in ants, let me tell you some interesting things about the survival strategies of these creatures,' his father said. 'In the rainy season, these creatures climb up the hill leaving the saturated earth beneath them. However, they don't all leave the bottom of the hill. The queen mother of the hill living in an ant-bud, which is well guarded by soldier-ants, would be left at the bottom of the hill. Because she is in a waterproof bud, she remains unaffected by the surrounding water. The soldier ants stationed in crevices above the sodden earth are also free of the water. In the dry season when heat torments the top of the hill, the ants will migrate to the bottom of the hill to escape the scorching heat at the top. These are the survival tricks of ants in their hill, my son,' the father said in an unvaried tone of casual discussions. 'However, all these tricks commit the ants to well-being only as long as the queen mother of the anthill is alive. The day she dies or is removed by men, that is the end of life in that anthill, as all the ants would flee the hill to build another. So, whenever you smash an anthill and find no ant inside, know that sometime ago, an ant queen mother was either removed from the empty hill or died there and the empty hill is her grave.'

Mallam Nuhu was speechless. The exposition by his father increased the stature of ants in his mind. 'Surely, man has a lot to learn from ants,' he thought.

At a later age, Mallam Nuhu came to this conclusion: knowledge and wisdom lay buried in anthills. The white man may build his schools for those yet to make this finding. As for him and others in possession of this truth, anthills embodied all that was required for human health and welfare. Was it unity for progress? Ants had it. Was it co-operation, a sense of community, a sense of fellowship? Ants had them in excess. Was it state security? Ants were the best security agents. Was it industry? Ants were the most industrious of God's creatures. Was it anonymity? Ants aspire to no fame. Dwelling on these themes, Mallam Nuhu came to this conclusion: if only men could come to a binding accord on the thriving values in an anthill, much of human misery would abate.

Ants' values on industry informed Mallam Nuhu's choice of a vocation. Day and night, ants were at work observing no sleep and knowing no rest; but ever on the move. The vocation of dankoli to him approximated the hyperactivity of the ants. He would have none of the indolence of a stationary tradesman.

It was his thinking that a man that attends not to his vocation daily is like a basket full of holes. Fortune comes in trickles not in mass. The best receptacle for it is a pan not a basket. This thinking, he called the sane truth. It was a truth he followed with abiding faith. In his vocation of dankoli, this truth propelled him to hyperactivity. It was constantly telling him that a good tradesman that takes advantage of good prices and large patronage is the one at his duty post not the one sleeping in his bed. That no tradesman knows the day or hour good fortune would come his way because the sun does not wake up from the west or with a disc on such a day. Since he cannot discern a lucky from an unlucky day, he must do his best everyday if he has a mind of keeping his date with fortune. His lack of prescience has condemned him to a life of servitude. Rarely does he escape this servitude. But if he serves his sentence faithfully, fortune, not only from his trade has no choice but to keep its date with him.

Besides the sane truth was what he called the mad truth. According to this truth, fortune is like a leaf in a whirlwind. Often, it is not the man who goes after it that catches it, but the ground that chases it not. Although he observed this truth, he followed it not, because he could also spot a lie in it. The lie was that the ground, in gaining the leaf, was merely receiving back that which it released to the wind. It gained no fortune. The wind had no choice in the matter but to return to *Mamman* what it took from *Mamman*. No man enjoys such ownership over fortune. Also, he followed not the mad truth because its tenets were not the tenets of the ant's school of industry which he was a graduate of.

Very early in life, he had this peculiar understanding of the character of money: money is a king that has no palace. Any courtier or palace politician of this king must seek the fortunes of his nomadic monarch in the fields. It is a god that has no shrine. Any worshipper of it must chase the providence of his desert god in the oracles of a camping deity. It is a maid without a home. Any suitor seeking the hand of this maid must be ready for night journeys across hills, rivers, and forests in search of his wandering maid.

It was his philosophy that if the elephant spends his days breaking trees, the hare should spend his breaking grass. He would not allow a man to surpass him in two departments of industry. If a man worked faster than him, he would work longer than him. If he walked faster than him, he would walk longer than him. If a man had more land than him, he would have more manure than him. It was a common saying on the lips of his customers that, 'Mallam Nuhu's trade might fail him by not turning in good profit; he would not fail it by putting in less time. It might be miserly in its remittance of reward; he would not answer that description towards his trade.'

Ants' security intelligence became his talisman, which he used to bind all adverse spirits, animals and human agencies, which might attack him in the course of his journeys across rivers and forests to take his wares to the homesteads of patronising villagers. Each time he was travelling through a big forest to a village to sell his articles, he would find an anthill at the beginning of the forest to commune with the guardian spirits that guarantee the security of an anthill in the forest. Placing his right foot on the hill, he would pray:

> Oh, you spirits that guarantee the security
> of an anthill standing alone in the forest; oh
> you ants the ancient security wizards that
> ensure the safety of queen mother ant. I am
> about to enter this forest, a lonely, weak
> human soul that cannot protect himself from
> the adversity of evil spirits, evil humans and
> vicious animals. I invoke your protection
> over myself. By your security, I will like a
> lonely anthill in the forest, be secured from
> all attacks by any agency as I walk through
> this forest, a harmless, innocent man, taking
> his trade to the next village.

After this supplication, he would remove the *laya* around his waist; lay it thrice on the anthill muttering incantations under his breath before tying it back on his waist again. Then, he would run round the anthill three times after which he would drop a bundle of fresh leaves on the anthill before moving on. Whenever he stood by an anthill, he could see in the ubiquity of anthills, the ubiquity of his trade and security.

On his arrival in a village, ants' sense of community and fellowship assumed his mind. The village was his village like the one he left behind. By all outward showing, he was on friendly terms with all the villagers; the young and the old, the friendly and the hostile, the courteous and the discourteous. Rarely was it heard that Mallam Nuhu quarrelled with a villager in the course of his trade. A man might call him like a prospective buyer only to dismiss him with a wave of the hand on his taking his wares to him. A woman might examine his articles like all buyers do, only to hiss and wave him away with her hand without buying anything. Mallam Nuhu rarely barked. He was as near agreeable to the vile as to the courteous. He had a prompt sense of patience that stood on guard of any flint of anger in him that ran the risk of being struck by trying customers. He had a belated sense of insult that rarely tried his patience. His prompt sense of patience and belated sense of insult coordinated themselves into a balm of rare friendship in this man of pleasing contours. In the villages he was known, it was a common saying that the day Mallam Nuhu barks, the fire of his patience would consume the source of his annoyance. When asked the source of his elastic patience, his reply was, 'the sheep is a patient animal. That is why what the dog is barking at now, the sheep had long seen but kept quiet.' For all the provocative antics of patronisers of his trade, he seldom broke ranks with ants' sense of community and fellowship.

In and outside his trade, he sought no attention or notice. Neither did he aspire for fame or applause. He was a being after means from the sweat of his brow without any thought for what people called greatness.

Often, he had occasions to compare his circumstances with those of his age mates that attended the white man's school. On such occasions, he saw himself as an authentic graduate of ants' natural school of life. This school taught a man not only to be industrious, but to be patient with the little or much his industry yielded for him. A stream of sufficiency flows through this school and he that was a graduate of the school had drunk from this stream. Living by the waters and tenets of this school, he came to be tolerant of circumstances others would have lamented their lot, and to be contented with means others would have despised.

His age mates that attended the white man's school, he saw as graduates of the white man's imitation of the ants' natural school of life. A stream of impatience and greed flows through this school. They that were graduates of the school had drunk from this stream. They had drunk the forbidden waters of greed and the wages were these: though getting more money than him, they did not enjoy his sufficiency. Eating much more than him, they remained hungry when he would have been vomiting from over-eating; drinking much more than him, they remained thirsty when he would have been drowned; wearing better clothes than him, they felt shabby when he would have felt like one adorned in royal robes. Their very souls were captives of avarice. They had eaten a racing hare, and by the words of the elders, had eaten a big race. They deserved his pity not his envy.

Chapter Three

Trading in Nakwana Village

Monday, May 5th

Nakwana village was in the western part of the Darakuwa Plateau. Situated in the recess of a valley, it was one of the villages that enjoyed the patronage of Mallam Nuhu's trade. In this village, he had good customers who always bought his articles. In the same village also, he used to come across rude customers who more often than not tasked the storehouse of his patience. The latter category of customers appeared to him to be more interested in drawing him into a quarrel than buying anything from him. If that was their desire, not often did they succeed in summoning his anger from its bottomless pit.

On May 5th, he arrived Nakwana village from Binjiri where he passed the previous night. From house to house, he moved; his trade jingle, *ga kayankoli!* moved ahead of him announcing his presence in the neighbourhood in regular intervals. He was omnipresent. One moment, his voice would be heard in western quarters of the village; the next moment, it would be heard in the eastern quarters. The echo of his voice extended his presence into quarters still far from his corporal presence. He needed neither loudspeaker nor advertisement promotions. He was his own loudspeaker and admass.

He was swift in his movement. Patronisers of his trade had to be swift too. Else, they would find he had long gone past their houses. By his electric movement and trade jingle pronounced in loud penetrating tones, he wired himself and patronisers of his trade to a fast-moving current. In all these, he maintained a regularity of stamina that fed steam to the regularity of his presence.

Presently, he was standing in front of the house of Alhaji Nasiru, a local rich man with a harem of four wives. Two of the wives were good customers of Mallam Nuhu while the other two belonged to the tribe of customers that sought his annoyance than his wares. As soon as he announced his presence at the gate of the house with *ga kayankoli*, three wives of Alhaji Nasiru came out to meet him. Two of these women were his good customers while the other belonged to the hostile category.

The two good customers bought two pairs of earrings each and paid for what they purchased. The other woman was yet to come to any decision about the article she wanted to buy. Item by item, she went over the entire articles in the tray picking each and examining it with a snobbish air. Holding an article by the tip of two fingers, she would give it a little shake while working her lips into a supercilious pout that in its silence eloquently declared, 'what rubbish!'

Mallam Nuhu stood by saying nothing. If he was angry, his face did not show it.

After she had taken her time going over his articles and apparently finding none worthy of her patronage, she gave voice to her pouted lips: 'Why is it that, you never seem to improve on the quality of your products? Year in, year out, you keep bringing the same worthless articles that go for less than half a penny in big towns. What do you take use for; fools?' she blared, glaring at him contemptuously. 'Well, man, you are wrong. We are not all fools. At least, I know I am not one. I lived in the city before I found myself in this bush with a pack of half-blind idiots who, all their lives, have not ventured beyond the next village. Away with your mess!' she cried, waving him away in the contemptuous manner a man might spurn a dog.

'Binta, mind the implication of what you say,' one of the other two women said, heatedly. 'How are you any better than any of us that had not lived in the city? Look, a prostitute should ....'

Binta slapped her across the face shouting, 'who you are calling a prostitute? Who are you calling a prostitute?'

The two women locked themselves into a fierce combat. A sheet of dust rose from the ground like a satanic cloud to envelope the two fighting women. Soon, a sharp, shrill cry rang out of their entangled bodies like the sound of the bell of death messenger. The other woman had bitten Binta on the neck. The fight gained a new ferocity.

Mallam Nuhu and the other woman who had stood looking like spellbound people stepped in to separate the two fighting women. Mallam Nuhu earned a kick on his leg for his pains. The other woman received a backhanded slap as a trophy for her effort to have peace be.

The two fighting women soon took to the ground, hitting, scratching and biting in an orgy of madness that celebrated the triumph of passion over reason. Mallam Nuhu and the other woman did not relent in their effort to separate the two women celebrating anger the only way it could be celebrated. Other people drawn to the scene by the scuffle appeared more interested in the sport it provided than its cessation. They stood watching, some laughing secretly while others by their complacency urged the two combatants on. They reminded Mallam Nuhu of a comic episode in his adolescent years. Two of his age mates were fighting in the night on a small playground and another age mate was holding a lantern for them so see where to land blows with maximum effect. He and the other woman again moved in to try to separate the fighting women that stuck to each other like disagreeable Siamese twins. This time they succeeded. Each of the women was bleeding from bite and scratch wounds inflicted by the other. Both of them had only their undies on. Their wrappers had since left them in the course of the fight. Shame took over. Each woman whirled round in frantic search for her wrapper to cover her near nudity. Only one wrapper lay on the ground half-covered by dust. It was that of Binta. But because it was half-buried in dust, its ownership was not easily detectable by the two desperate combatants. They both dashed for it taking hold of different ends of the wrapper. For a moment, they stood glaring at each other from opposite ends of the wrapper held between them. An imminent second round of the fight charged the atmosphere.

But Ahaji Nasiru's other wife enforced a truce. She handed over to Mallam Nuhu's good customer her wrapper, which she had picked up from the ground in the course of the fight to save it from being soiled or even torn by the combatants. The combatant woman let go of the wrapper in contention and collected her own from the other woman. But Binta, the troublesome woman, was not finished with them yet. She flew at the woman giving the wrapper. But the woman backed off laughing at her.

Peace settled on the scene like a vulture on the scene of a departed battle.

Mallam Nuhu was sad that his trade should provide the occasion for a fracas like this. Though he suspected the two women had scores to settle far removed from his trade, he was nonetheless sad that his trade should provide the opportunity for the settlement of such scores.

'How do I trade in this house?' he wondered.

'Do not bring your worthless wares to this house again!' Binta shouted from the threshold of the vestibule where she stood looking sullenly at Mallam Nuhu.

Mallam Nuhu was shocked by what Binta said. Was she reading his mind? '*Allahu Akbar*!' he recited quietly to himself. 'But I make a lot of sales in this house. Who will buy what my good customers here buy?' he thought, despairingly.

'Go away Mallam Nuhu, go. The devil will buy from you!' Binta cried waving him away.

'The devil surely lives in this woman,' he said to himself as he scampered from the house. What! Nhm… But my good customers!'

'May you sell all your wares in the next forest!' Binta shouted after him.

'*A'uzubillahi!*' Mallam Nuhu cried.

May we never sell all our articles in one trip, was a common expression of goodwill among yankoli. This saying was informed by the fact that it was near impossible for a dankoli to sell all his articles in a single trip, no matter the patronage he enjoyed. This was because dankoli had so many assorted articles that could not possibly be purchased all in one trip. The realization of this fact led yankoli to a conclusion that only in three circumstances may dankoli *sell* all his wares in a single trip: He might be attacked by armed robbers who would take away his wares; he might be overpowered by a flood he had waded into; and if he was a womanizer, he might be caught with somebody's wife putting him on the run for his life. These being the only circumstances yankoli knew they could *sell* all their articles in a single trip, an address to dankoli that may he sell all his wares was taken to mean, may any of these misfortunes befall him. It was a salutation of ill-will no dankoli took lightly with anybody.

I have become a thing of shoddy treatment by women, Mallam Nuhu thought. God, you have not been fair to me. *A'uzubillahi,'* he muttered, fearfully. 'God, have mercy on me.'

From Alhaji Nasiru's house, he hurried away from that quarter of the village to another quarter. Apart from the fact that he wanted to put a distance between him and the unfortunate incident, most of the women in that neighbourhood, whom he would have taken his wares to, had been drawn to the scene of the fight and he could see they were not as interested in his wares as in the vicious gossips that had divided the crowd which the fight attracted into small gossip groups.

In the southern quarter, he stopped by the house of Mallam Amani. The only woman of the house bought *tozali* and two bangles from him. Mallam Amani who in the rainy season was prone to pneumonia attack, bought garlic.

He moved to the next house. Sabo the owner of this house bought *tazargade* an evil spirit-expelling herb, which Mallam Nuhu used to buy from the Tuaregs for his trade. Recently, Sabo was being tormented by the crying of his little children each night – a development he suspected to be caused by evil spirits. Because of this, he has not known proper sleep for the past four nights. The herb, a powdery, brown substance would be poured into live charcoal and the incense generated by it would drive away the evil spirits tormenting his children and he and his household would know sleep again. Two of his wives came out. One bought a pair of earrings. The other, like Binta the quarrelsome wife of Alhaji Nasiru, did not seem to be too interested in buying anything. Nevertheless, she wasted his time by going over all his articles only to hiss and re-enter the house without a word to him. He picked his articles and moved to the next house, and after that, the next.

By evening, he had gone through the whole village almost house by house. He headed for the house of Dogari where he used to sleep whenever he was passing the night in Nakwana village. On his way, he remembered what happened in Alhaji Nasiru's house earlier in the day. 'No, I will not sleep in this village today,' he said, suddenly. 'I don't want anybody to invite me to an inquiry. I am a lonely man of peace like the lonely ants in the forest. I want no trouble of an inquiry.' Saying this, he changed course and headed to the nearby village of Shuruba, a popular Maguzawa village in the Darakuwa Plateau.

Chapter Four

Fortune Reared her Head

Many years ago, at the peak of one rainy season, Mallam Nuhu was on his way from Shuruba village to Yakaje village when a need to relieve himself took hold of him with an urgency that rushed him into the bush on the quick. Placing his wares beside him, he squatted behind a shrub. He was still in the business of meeting the pleasures of his bowels when his wandering eyes spotted something white under a shrub to his right. Half standing, half stooping Mallam Nuhu with his trousers on his knees shuffled to the shrub and peered at the white appearance. Behold, it was the *taurikiki* mushrooms that in those days equated the meat of a lion in the estimation of the villagers who enjoyed its delicate taste and knew its rich nourishment. Indeed, *taurikiki* mushrooms were the lion of all edible mushrooms. They had no compare and were rare to find. When found, they were cooked and shared to neighbours by the person who found them the same way the meat of a lion was shared by a hunter who killed that animal. Finding the mushrooms was not only celebrated because of their delicacy, but because of a belief that whoever found the mushrooms would soon be rich. On seeing the mushrooms, Mallam Nuhu was jubilant. He put out his hand to pull out one of the mushrooms and his eyes fell on a small bundle of *bunsuru fegge* grass that was partly dry and partly fresh. Mallam Nuhu shrank away from the taurikiki mushroom as he would from a snake.

Bunsuru fegge grass is grass with long blades used as a purgative to chase away ants from farmlands and residences by farmers and houseowners. Salt and potash mixed in water were also used for the same end. But perhaps the most potent ants' purgative was the water of *fidda firutsa* – a poisonous tree. The moment the water of this tree was poured on an anthill, the ants in the hill, even without the hill being dug out, would all perish in a moment.

The presence of a bundle of *bunsuru fegge* grass beside the mushrooms meant the bundle of grass was placed there by the first person who found the mushrooms. The practice was, whenever a person found *taurikiki* mushrooms just budding from the ground, yet to fully grow, he may drop a bundle of leaves or some other forest growth beside the mushrooms. Such leaves or forest growth were adequate notice to anyone finding the mushrooms later that they were already someone else's property. The leaves or other forest growth remained by the side of the mushrooms until they achieved full growth. Then the owner comes to claim his property.

'Whoever has found you and placed this evil grass beside you must be an evil man,' Mallam Nuhu said leaving the mushrooms to squat again behind another shrub. It was an abomination for him to pick the mushrooms, which had attained full maturity and were likely to be picked that day or the following day by whoever first found them. 'It is my misfortune and his fortune, though he does not mean well,' he whispered bitterly. 'What fortune is mine? Where is it?'

When he finished relieving himself, he regained the path again. Near a small stream, his right foot stumbled on something that felt like a stone. He lurched forward then regained his balance. He looked back to see what he stumbled on. He found himself staring at a thunderbolt. He could not believe his eyes. Surely, they must be seeing things; it must be a common stone that looks like the precious rain stone. He put down his wares and picked up the thunderbolt. The feel of it in his palms and its weight more than the judgment of his eyes told him he was holding a thunderbolt. 'Every man and his fortune!' he cried. A dove perching nearby, startled by the racket of his voice, flew up into the air and skirted off. He looked at the sun. 'There is no disc on the sun today!' he shouted and beamed at the open sky. 'What a day!'

The thunderbolt was believed to have several medicinal properties. A woman in labour may be given water into which the rain stone had been soaked. After drinking such water, her labour and delivery were likely to be less painful and perilous. With the rain stone in one's possession, one was immune from thunder strikes. When a man licked the bolt and spoke to his fellow, the voice of the man who licked the rain stone, like thunder, strikes fear into the heart of his fellow who must oblige him. The Maguzawas who refused to accept Islam, used the rain stone to bring rain and to stop it. They used it to make their crops grow and yield better and to diminish the harvest of their enemies.

'The way fortune is crossing my path today, I will not be surprised if I happen upon *jatau* today,' Mallam Nuhu whispered to himself full of gaiety.

Jatau in the native Hausa mind was something of a mermaid. It was a flaming appearance often sighted at night at a distance, but also capable of being sighted in the daytime. As a man moved towards *jatau*, it disappeared to appear at a distance again changing character and shape and flaming even more brilliantly. If the man became afraid and ran away, he became mad. But if he was a man of courage or strong in medicine and persisted in pursuing the flaming appearance, eventually it would surrender to him and he would become quite rich. Most rich people of ancient time were said to be men who had the heart, braved the odds, pursued *jatau* and gained its favour. *Jatau* did not only bring wealth, it brought beauty to children yet unborn by whoever was its favourite. Rich and exceptionally handsome people, if they were also light complexion, were incarnation of the flaming appearance and were therefore called Jatau.

Mallam Nuhu removed his inner wear, wrapped the thunderbolt inside it and moved on.

What was he to do with the thunderbolt? he kept asking himself. If he were a farmer, perhaps he would have put it to better economic use. As a village tradesman, the most use he could put it to was to use it as a shield against thunder and other adverse forces as he moved from village to village hawking his wares. This use appeared to him of less value compared to the high value of the rain stone. Besides, he already had anthills out there in the forest, which he did not have to carry about with him; why go about with a thunderbolt raising suspicion and burdening himself? What was he to do with it then? The rain stone was not a commercial article sold and purchased in the market. Neither was it rented or hired out for a fee. Still, he felt there was no reason he could not sell or hire out the rain stone if he wished; and he wished to rent it out to the Maguzawas who had so much use for it than the Hausas. Having made this resolution, he changed course and began moving back to Shuruba village, which he earlier left.

He arrived the village towards evening and went straight to the house of Tambuwal the *Sarkin Noma* of Shuruba village. But Tambuwal was not at home when he got to his house. He was in his farm and would only return in five days' time. Mallam Nuhu asked of direction to the farm. Tambuwal's wife gave him. It turned out that Tambuwal was quite near where he found the thunderbolt and a little knowledge of this fact would have sav+ed him the toil of going back to

Shuruba village. Without wasting time and without telling Tambuwal's wife why he was looking for her husband, he started walking back the way he came. He must see Tambuwal and rent the rain stone to him.

Mallam Nuhu arrived Tambuwal's farm towards sunset. Tambuwal was alone in the farm. He was stirring with a long stick a big fire he had made. Each time he stuck the stick into the fire, the flames seemed to giggle before spitting out incandescent sparks. After stirring the fire with the stick for a while, he used the same stick to poke at yam he was roasting in the fire. Though Mallam Nuhu has heard about him, he had never met him in person. But the description of the farm he was given and the image of Tambuwal he had in his mind, matched the farm he stood in and the man he stood before.

'Well done,' he greeted Tambuwal.

'Well done, Mallam Nuhu,' Tambuwal answered with a lot of warm and cheer. 'To what do I owe your presence in my farm this evening?'

Mallam Nuhu's face light up in surprise. 'This trade,' he murmured. To be known by the *Sarkin Noma* of Shuruba a village he rarely visited was astounding.

'Should I or should I not,' Mallam Nuhu suddenly found himself wondering whether or not he should rent the rain stone to Tambuwal. Though he had long decided to lease the thunderbolt to Tambuwal, now that he was before the farmer, he began wondering if he should. A disturbing doubt like an uncleared mucus in his throat was warning him not to. The doubt was pressing on his mind the high esteem, bordering on veneration, which Maguzawas had for the rain stone. It was telling him that there was no knowing what mischief Tambuwal's mind would tend to once he had possession of the rain stone. He may simply deny he gave him the thunderbolt or claimed he bought it from him. Yet, this high esteem of the Maguzawas for the rain stone was the reason he wanted to lease it to Tambuwal for good returns. Since Tambuwal as *Sarkin Noma* would put it to good use and increase his crop yields, he would pay him handsomely for it.

Tambuwal, seeing Mallam Nuhu undecided about what was his mission in his farm, asked him to sit down and warm himself by the fire while they wait for the yam he was roasting to roast.

Mallam Nuhu sat down. Hunger sleeping uneasily in his stomach sat up and demanded for food.

Soon the yam was ready for eating and Tambuwal using the same stick he used to poke the yam to feel its progress through the roasting process, pulled it out of the fire. After dusting the yam with his hands, which were as united in colour and dirt with the yam as the yam was with the heat that roasted it, he used a knife to scrape it clean for eating. Between mouthfuls, he asked Mallam Nuhu how trade was.

'Rainy season, the season your trade prospers is the low season for my trade,' Mallam Nuhu replied also between mouthfuls of roasted yam that drained all the dews of the mouth leaving deserts in its wake. 'In the rainy season, we walk the paths as a hen scratches the winnow ground, out of habit than out of any excitement we get from grains we turn up. Sometimes, I get to a village to find the people of the village relocated to their farms. Like now, I was in your house and was told you were in your farm along the path I followed to your house. You can see how my trade can be frustrating in the rainy season. Even when you find people in a village, they would tell you they had no money to buy your articles because money has gone back to the soil. Even your debtors tell you that. What can you do?'

'When a man is looked for the way you have looked for me, such a man must have committed an offence. What is my offence?' Tambuwal asked Mallam Nuhu with a smile that reached the village tradesman.

Tambuwal appearing to be a good man of good humour, Mallam Nuhu decided to lease the thunderbolt to him. 'Shortly after noon today; not far from where we are, I stumbled on something I thought was a stone only to find on looking down, it is this,' he said, showing Tambuwal the thunderbolt.

On seeing the rain stone, Tambuwal's face became pale with envy and dark with a nameless anger; but quickly regained its amiability before Mallam Nuhu whose eyes were fastened on the rain stone looked up to see how he was taking the sight of the rain stone. When he looked up, what he saw was Tambuwal's laughing face.

'About the time you said you found the thunderbolt, I was returning from the stream where I had gone to get drinking water when I heard somebody shout as if in joy; were you the one who shouted?' Tambuwal who had heard the shout of Mallam Nuhu and thought of investigating it but changed his mind, asked.

'So, you heard me?' Mallam Nuhu asked, shocked. To think Tambuwal he had spent most of the day trying to find actually was so near him as to hear him shout when the need for his looking for the farmer arose was quite stunning. 'I have actually been looking for Bage's sickle,'* he chuckled.

'Yes, you have,' Tambuwal replied the smile pasted on the rough walls of his rigorous face remaining where it was pasted. His mind beyond the smile was very busy. 'Is this what people mean when they say hot pursuit of wealth

---

* *In Hausa folklore, Bage was a man who after returning home from the bush with grass he had gone there to cut, started looking for the sickle he cut the grass with. He searched everywhere at home but could not find the sickle. He went back to the bush where he cut the grass and searched everywhere but could not find the sickle. He came back home restless and miserable. He went to his room and lay down to rest, if he could rest. Then he felt something pricking him in his waist and behold it was the sickle he had spent most of his day looking for. All the while it was by his trousers' waistband where he had stuck it. In anger, he flung out the sickle with a curse.*

does not bring it?' he asked himself. For the past three years, his crops had been failing because of witchweeds that had started growing on his farms. Year in, year out, he pulled out the witchweeds and burned them, but they would appear the following year in larger numbers than the previous year. A thunderbolt was fire from the sky that consumed the fire of the earth including witchweeds. He had been looking for a thunderbolt to burn out the witchweeds of his farms to no avail. Believing so much in the potency of a thunderbolt to burn out the witchweeds in his farms and improve their fertility and the yield of his crops, there was nowhere he had not looked for the rain stone. Trees known to have been struck by thunder many years ago, he had dug around them hoping to turn up the agricultural talisman, but in vain. He had even gone to the bizarre length of hoping that thunder strikes a tree near his farm and if it meant his turning the earth by that tree upside down and shaking it for the rain stone in the manner he would his trousers for his snuff bottle, he would do so. To think all this while a thunderbolt was lying by the path beside his farm only to be found by a nomadic tradesman who knew not its powers made him sick with irritation. And now without any effort of his, a hungry hen, not knowing it is roosting on a bundle of millet, was offering the bundle to him. Well, as at yet he couldn't say it was offering it to him. But whatever eventually be the reason of Mallam Nuhu looking for him with the rain stone, that he would not allow him leave the farm with the rain stone, he was sure.

'Why have you been looking for Bage's sickle?' he asked Mallam Nuhu whose mind also has been very busy. There was no going back,' he told himself firmly. He would lease the thunderbolt to Tambuwal; but for how much and for how long? His economic mind told him that valuable objects like the thunderbolt were to be leased for a fortune and for a short period less the lessee begins to harbour sinister ideas of ownership.

'I want to lease my thunderbolt to you,' Mallam Nuhu said.

Tambuwal thought he had a stress in Mallam Nuhu's voice on the word *my* and it angered him, but he did not show his annoyance. Between him before whose farm the rain stone laid for how long, he could not tell, and these wandering *Bororo* who only moments ago stumbled on it, who is more entitled to say, *my* he thought angrily. Shouldn't I even tell him the thunderbolt is mine, washed to the path by rainwater? he wondered. But the lie of such a claim appeared to him as soon as the thought crossed his mind and he swiftly renounced it. There are many ways to skin a rat, he consoled himself.

'For how much do you want to lease it to me?' he asked, collecting the thunderbolt from Mallam Nuhu. He had seen a thunderbolt only once in his life, but he knew even by the shape and

complexion of the object in Mallam Nuhu's hand
that it is a thunderbolt. Holding it in his right palm,
he hurled it a couple of times into the air swooping
it up each time it was falling. The feel of it on his
palm each time was thrilling beyond measure. His
excitement, like group laughter, engulfed Mallam
Nuhu.

'Three pounds a year,' said *Samu* who forgot
he had not found *jatau*

'Mallam Nuhu!'

'What did I say?'

'Better. How much are you leasing it to me?
But wait; why not sell it to me? As a village
tradesman, you will never need it.'

This was when Mallam Nuhu should have
recalled his offer and left if Tambuwal would
allow him leave with the rain stone, but he did not.
Instead, he said, 'that is not what life has taught
me. What we think we don't need today, tomorrow
all our lives may depend on it. I can only lease it
out.'

'How much are you leasing it then?'

'Three Shillings a year,' Mallam Nuhu who
had since recollected himself after wild
expectations seized him, said with levelled
certitude.

'That is not too high a ransom for this
generous element,' Tambuwal said, hugging the
rain stone as the devil might hug a witch. 'But
won't you consider coming down a little?'

'Ransom; what do you mean by ransom?'

'Sorry, I meant to say lease.'

'I cannot come down a little,' Mallam Nuhu wondering if he was not throwing away the rain stone for peanuts said with a finality that bore a ring of regret. 'The lease is only for a year and would be reviewed in subsequent years.'

'That's OK by me,' Tambuwal said. 'For how many years would you be renewing your lease to me?'

Mallam Nuhu had no intention of leasing the thunderbolt to anybody for more than two years. He intended to keep moving to new grounds in search of better offers instead of getting stuck with one lessee who might begin to have phoney ideas. Who knows, this could be his *jatau;* after all, *jatau* comes to his favourites in different forms. But he did not say this to Tambuwal. To Tambuwal he said, 'I will rent it to you for as long as you want to hire it. You know everything of dankoli is for sale.'

'I know. That was why I said you should sell it to me.'

'Leasing is a form of sale.'

'We have a deal then. Three Shillings a year. When will you come for the money?'

'When you need the thunderbolt,' Mallam Nuhu said, stretching his left hand to collect the thunderbolt from Tambuwal still hugging it.

But Tambuwal did not extend the bolt to his outstretched hand, which hung limply in the air for a while before falling to his side. Perhaps, if he had known the thoughts going through Tambuwal's mind then, he wouldn't have extended the hand. Tambuwal was thinking of killing him with his hoe or even with the thunderbolt and possessing the rain stone for good. But his thoughts were arrested by the presence of Makama in his farm less than a stone throw away from his farm. Makama would surely hear Mallam Nuhu's death throes and rush in to know what was amiss; unless he was ready to kill Makama as well! His mind baulked at the prospect of becoming a serial killer when he had not killed before. If Mallam Nuhu were not intent on having his thunderbolt back, he would have noticed the sinister expression on Tambuwal's face when the latter thought of killing him and looked round for his hoe.

'You must be joking to think I will allow you leave this farm with this bolt when I had done strange things to find it without success,' he said, issuing the most becoming smile a man of savage intent can issue.

Again, Mallam Nuhu was taken in by Tambuwal's smile, but not to the extent of leaving the rain stone with the farmer without having been paid for it. 'Well, you may keep it if you are that desperate to have it,' he said. 'But I must be paid what we have agreed; and we must call the man over there,' he said pointing at Makama in his farm, 'to be a witness to this transaction so that neither of us would later say what was not.'

'I have two Shillings with me here,' Tambuwal said, bringing out two Shillings from the pocket of his shirt hung on a tree stump behind him. 'You can have these two Shillings and later come for the remaining Shilling in my house or this farm if we agree on a date.'

Mallam Nuhu agreed and Makama was called to witness the transaction. When the transaction was concluded, it was too late for Mallam Nuhu to move on. He decided to pass the night in Tambuwal's farmhouse.

While he slept in the night, several times Tambuwal driven by an obsession of owning the rain stone went to stand darkly over him either with his hoe held high in the air or with the rain stone in his two hands. Each time, he was arrested by the forbidding presence of Makama who knew Mallam Nuhu was passing the night in his farm. However, if the matter had rested only with the presence of Makama, with his increased obsession with the rain stone, he would have done something about Makama that night. But the matter did not rest with Makama alone. There was his wife to think of. She directed Mallam Nuhu to the Farm. What of other countless people Mallam Nuhu might have met on his way to the farm and informed of his destination? Mallam Nuhu was a celebrity in the land. There was no telling who he didn't see or talked to, but who saw him entering his farm. Each time he went to stand over Mallam Nuhu with the hoe or thunderbolt in his hands, the risk he was running by killing this nomadic trader appeared higher than he previously thought. Yet, he wouldn't give up trying until towards dawn when fearing that Mallam Nuhu might be sleeping light, he went to his bed and lay down. He had not found where his ribs would come to comfortable terms with his bed of corn stalks when he heard Mallam Nuhu coughed. The cough was followed by a string of indescribable movements, which ended with him sitting up on his bed. He had woken up and would not sleep again that night. In the morning, he bade farewell to Tambuwal with the understanding he was to come for the balance of his money a fortnight.

Tambuwal left behind, thought it was time he went to pluck his mushrooms, which he felt must have ripened enough to be plucked without sacrificing any of their taste or quantity to premature picking. To delay further would be taking unnecessary chances in an age and time people were thinking more with their stomachs than with their heads. Mallam Nuhu was not gone for long when he set off after him. He found the mushrooms as he left them and ripened as he expected. But he could see somebody else has been there after he was last there. The footprints of the fellow were there for him to see. 'So long as he didn't pick my *taurikiki,* what do I care?' he said, bending down to pick the mushrooms into a big basket he had brought with him.

Chapter Five

The Backside of Greed

By agreement, Mallam Nuhu was to meet Tambuwal in his farm and collect the balance of his money. On the appointed day, Mallam Nuhu set out with his wares from Talabiya village to Tambuwal's farm full of hope and plans of what to do with the money when he gets it. He would buy more wares and put away more money for the future. Prosperity like a seductive whore whispered into his ears and he was happy. He found Tambuwal in the farm. After an exchange of greetings, he told Tambuwal he had come for the money as agreed.

'Which money are you talking about?' Tambuwal asked with the right measure of surprise in voice and countenance that would make anyone who did not know of the transaction wonder why Mallam Nuhu was springing something new on a man who knew nothing of what he was saying. Indeed, even Mallam Nuhu for a moment wondered if he was talking to the wrong person and not Tambuwal. He looked round and was sure he was standing in Tambuwal's farm. He looked well at the man before him and was sure the man was Tambuwal who he leased his thunderbolt to.

'Tambuwal, have you forgotten that two weeks ago I leased a thunderbolt to you for three Shillings a year out of which you gave me two

Shillings and I am to come for the balance today?' he asked in a voice that left nothing of his amazement.

'My friend I don't know you; in fact, I have never seen you before. As for your thunderbolt, perhaps you might have sold it along with an earring or a bangle only to forget and think you have rented it to me. Why on earth should I rent a thunderbolt? Who has ever rented a rain stone? Is it a farmland to be rented?' he asked, laughing; then all at once became fierce looking.

'*Sarkin Noma,* if this a joke, I think you have rode it too far and should come down and pay me so that I proceed on my trade and allow you concentrate on yours,' he said, sweat breaking out on his forehead and tremors breaking his voice into jots.

'You have made the point,' Tambuwal said. 'You need to go and attend to your trade as much as I desire to be left alone to concentrate on mine,' he said, losing all pretence of civility and taking on the immoral look of a man who had damned conscience.

Mallam Nuhu not liking Tambuwal's bearing towards him retreated some metres away from the farmer his eyes more on Tambuwal's hand with the hoe than on any other part of his body. 'Well, since we didn't seal this transaction alone,' he said, 'Makama is there to bear me witness.' He started walking towards Makama's farm taking care to look back now and then. He entered the farm and looked round, but there was no sign of Makama. He called out, but only the echo of his voice replied him. 'Where could Makama be?' he wondered in distress. As he stood thinking of what to do, a young man came running into the farm holding a calabash full of water he had gone to the stream to fetch. The young man was crying.

'Baba, why do you come calling the dead pouring salt on fresh wounds,' the young man wept, cutting the most pathetic image Mallam Nuhu had ever beheld.

'Who is dead?' he asked the young man.

'My father.'

'You mean Makama?'

'Yes.'

'*La ila a ilahuwa Muhammdu Rasulilah*! When did this happen?'

'Eleven days ago.'

'What killed him?'

'We can't say precisely. All we know is that he died after drinking gruel with Sarkin Noma in his farm.'

Mallam Nuhu became dizzy. He sat down facing the direction Tambuwal, if he had a mind of paying them a visit might come through. 'Was it the first time Sarkin Noma invited him for such meal?'

'No. We have a habit of eating in each other's farms now and then,' replied the young man.

Despite the report of routine, Mallam Nuhu had no doubt Tambuwal killed Makama the only witness to their agreement. If he would have had doubt before, the murderous look on Tambuwal's face when he broached the issue of the agreement moments ago removed such doubt.

'What are you to Makama?'

'I am his son.'

'What is your name?'

'Babe.'

'Babe, what did your father tell you before he died?' Mallam Nuhu asked and immediately regretted asking the question; for it was an improper question liable to be misunderstood. A person's father would have told him many things before his death that are not and should not be the business of anybody.

Babe must have felt the same way for he did not say anything.

'Sorry for that question,' Mallam Nuhu said. 'I meant to ask you, did your father tell you anything about an agreement between a dankoli and Sarkin Noma?'

'No; he didn't tell me such thing,' Babe answered for the first time taking interest in Mallam Nuhu's tray and the wares in it; 'are you dankoli?'

'Yes.'

'What agreement did you have with Sarkin Noma that my father witnessed?' Babe asked, earnestly.

'It was an agreement that I would give Sarkin Noma one Shilling for his honey that I bought, but couldn't pay,' Mallam Nuhu lied. He had advised himself not to endanger the young man's life by telling him about the agreement. He had already done enough harm to him by involving his father in his transaction with Tambuwal – an involvement that might have caused him his life. 'Take heart and bear with fortitude what has happened,' he said after a long silence. 'May Allah have mercy on his gentle soul.'

'Amen.'

'I shall be seeing you again,' he said, leaving the young man.

He went back to Tambuwal.

'What did you do to Makama?' Mallam Nuhu asked Tambuwal fuming with rage.

'Mind what you say and to who you say it?' Tambuwal said, his words escaping through his teeth with a swish that made Mallam Nuhu thought of a hissing snake.

'I said, why did you kill Makama because you want to own a thunderbolt? Why didn't you kill me that night and take it? That night I saw you in my dream standing over me with a hoe; why didn't you crush my head, but instead killed an innocent man?' he asked, tearfully.

'If you don't leave now, I will do what I couldn't do that night,' Tambuwal said, advancing on Mallam Nuhu with his hoe held high in the air.

If before he looked bestial, he looked bloodthirsty now.

Mallam Nuhu retreated from the untamed man; then took to his heels.

Tambuwal stood where he was hissing and stamping his feet.

Chapter Six

An Honest Man swore by God

After running away from Tambuwal, Mallam Nuhu headed to the shrine of the Chief Priest of Shuruba Hajo Maiguza to report what happened between him and Tambuwal and request Tambuwal be summoned to swear by Aradu the god of thunder among the Maguzawa.

Though Mallam Nuhu was a Moslem, he knew Maguzawa who were mainly animists preferred to swear by any god other than Aradu the tribe's god of thunder. To a Maguzawa man, there was nothing more deadly than swearing by Aradu. As sure as heat comes from the sun, anyone who swore falsely by Aradu would not live beyond a rainy season before he was struck by thunder. But the futility of making Tambuwal swear by the god of thunder suddenly struck Mallam Nuhu. With my thunderbolt in his possession thunder cannot strike him even if he swore by Aradu, unless he is not carrying the rain stone with him, he thought. And why would he not carry it knowing he had sworn by the god of thunder?' A drop of sweat fell off his face. But there are chances he will sometimes forget and not carry it; indeed, there are inconveniences that will make him not to always carry it. For instance, he cannot conveniently carry it and till the soil. Indeed, he can become careless and not carry it. The god is known to make people who swore by him careless so that he can easily strike them. His face became a shade brighter. These thoughts, like the weeding fingers of an old woman exercised to weeding, weeded the doubts that were about choking his decision to petition the chief priest of Aradu that Tambuwal be made to swear by the god.

The chief priest was not in the shrine when he arrived there. He had closed for the day according to his page a lad of about fourteen years whom life had thrust a begging bowl into his hands and was still wondering what to do with it. Mallam Nuhu left and returned the following day at the time he was told he would meet the Chief Priest. The chief priest a short rotund man who fitted into the small shrine like a snail into its shell was in the shrine with all the dignity and airs of his office. While his dignity was sober, his imperial air roamed about the small shrine like a prancing cock.

Mallam Nuhu narrated to the chief priest what happened between him and Tambuwal from beginning to end, adding nothing and omitting nothing. He told him of his suspicion concerning Makama's death and requested Tambuwal be summoned to swear by Aradu.

'If what you told me is true, because I wonder when people started leasing thunderbolt, one of my own has done you a great wrong that cannot go unpunished,' the chief priest said with a sense of justice that felt insulted by the reported perfidy. 'But, on your part, are you prepared to swear by Aradu you gave him the thunderbolt?'

For a moment, Mallam Nuhu was tempted to say he would swear by the god of thunder, but quickly renounced the temptation. If he swore by Aradu and his fellow Moslems got to hear of such woeful act, and he was sure the bush telegraph would take it to them, he would be treated as having recanted Islam and the consequences were more than what he would lose if he did not recover the thunderbolt from Tambuwal. 'No, I cannot swear by Aradu,' he said.

'Then you don't know Maguzawa custom,' the chief priest said. 'Maguzawa do not swear by Aradu on the petition of a man who cannot swear by the god. The god will not honour a man who will not honour him.'

'What do I swear by?' Mallam Nuhu wandered through myriad paths in his mind looking for a god to swear by. Between Allah and Jiba, he tarried for a while before settling on Allah and swiftly swore by this God before his mind cast him asunder to other gods, he knew not to what harm or good.

'I swear by *Allah Subuhanna Wata'ala* that my thunderbolt is with Sarkin Noma of Shuruba. I swear by Allah Subuhanna Wata'ala that Sarkin Noma Tambuwal killed Makama so that he does not testify that I leased him my thunderbolt. Allah who sees and knows all things will avenge Makama and me,' he said, his hands raised towards heaven. Without saying goodbye to the chief priest, he left the shrine and proceeded on his trade.

Chapter Seven

An Old Woman told a Tale

Tuesday, May 6th

In Shuruba – Tambuwal's village, lived Hauwa an old woman and good customer of Mallam Nuhu. She was so fond of him that in her younger days, when she still had use for his trinkets, she would not buy any from another trader but from him. In those days, whenever he came to her village and she had money, she would buy as many trinkets as would last her his next trip to her village. While she exercised a strong persuasion on him to frequent the village for his trade, his aversion for Tambuwal after the latter cheated him of his thunderbolt sometimes inclined him against going to the village. Whenever he was going to the village, he found himself caught up in *should I* or *should I not* persuasion and dissuasion. More often than not, Hauwa's pull always overwhelmed his loathing of Tambuwal. Because of her patronage, and friendly disposition towards him, he kept going to Shuruba village in reciprocation of her goodwill long after age made a difference in her patronage of his wares. Though age had severed her commercial ties with most of his wares, he could see it had not severed her goodwill for him.

When he fled Nakwana for Shuruba village after the fracas between Nasiru's wives, it was Hauwa's house he first went to. While there, the old woman told him a tale that reinforced his faith in the potency of anthill's security ritual. After he had announced his presence at the gate of Hauwa's house with *assalamum alaikum* salutation, a small boy came out to meet him. On seeing Mallam Nuhu, the boy ran back into the house shouting, 'Iya, Iya! It is your dankoli; dankoli, Iya.'

'My dankoli? Are you sure it is Mallam Nuhu, my dankoli?' Hauwa asked in an excited voice, getting up from the small stool she sat on in her room. She walked to the gate as fast as her age would allow. At the gate, she squinted and peered at Mallam Nuhu, but was not sure he was the one.

'It is Mallam Nuhu, Iya, your dankoli,' he added, smiling at her. His voice seemed structured to achieve what her eyes could not.

'Oh, Mallam Nuhu; so, you are still alive? Hmm ... ho ho ho! The tale I heard of the conspiracy against you made me think they had killed you.'

'Which tale, and which people conspired against me?' he asked in a voice that often did not hurry to excitement.

'Hmmm ... Mallam Nuhu,' she grunted again, drawing her words heavily as if in a tug-of-war with somebody over them. 'It was a terrifying tale when I heard it and its terror has been with me, haunting my memory of you till now. Please come and sit inside the vestibule and let me tell you the danger I was made to believe you were under.'

Mallam Nuhu followed her into the vestibule and sat down.

'You remember the last time you came to this village?' she began.

'Yes, I remember. It is about four months ago.'

'Good. It is about that time,' Hauwa said. 'Perhaps you will also remember you took a gruel from a Fulani woman under the mango tree by the village square.'

'Yes.'

'You can also remember that as you were leaving the Fulani woman, I arrived the place and you even bought gruel for me from the same woman?'

'Yes,' Mallam Nuhu answered, wondering where all these questions were leading to.

'Fine. Sometime after you left and after I finished taking my gruel, the Fulani woman told me what she overheard some three giants saying about you.'

'Who were they and what were they saying about me?' Mallam Nuhu asked eager to hear what remained of the story the old woman was telling him.

'Well, I don't know the people. But whoever they were, they were evil people that conspired to waylay you, kill you and make away with your money on your way from this village to

Honaka village. So, the Fulani woman told me. First, she asked me what I am to you and I said you are my dankoli and close acquaintance. She then told me she overheard three giants discussing while you were taking your gruel that this dankoli has made a lot of sales today. We will waylay the bastard in the Barkada forest, kill the useless thing and make away with his money.'

'*A' uzubillah*i!' Mallam Nuhu chanted. 'But why should men plot such evil?' he asked, rhetorically.

'When she told me the story, I was angry she didn't tell me earlier for me to warn you. I felt sad as I gave you up to a certain death. Since then, I have been making inquiries of anyone who might have seen or heard about you. But nobody I asked seemed to have either seen or heard about you. No news of you, only for you to appear today. Oh Nuhu!'

'Iya, I am your dankoli. Be happy. Nothing happened to me and *Insha Allah* nothing will happen to me. I will only die as destined by Almighty Allah and not by three giants, whatever their strength. So, if tomorrow anybody comes and tells you he overheard *yan dabba* or *yan tauri* conspiring to kill Mallam Nubu dankoli, fear nothing. I can take care of myself in the midst of such hounds,' he said in a voice that seemed to assure him as much as her.

Hauwa nodded her head meaningfully. The fixation of her eyes on one spot, the manner she nodded her head and the humming sound from her nose combined to convey a new impression and insight she had about Mallam Nuhu. 'Before weeds grow in the land of a man …' she said after moment's silence.

'They have already grown in the heart of the man who owns the land,' Mallam Nuhu completed for her.

'The weeds in his heart …'

'Are the weeds in the land.'

'Let the evil seeds grow only in the fields of the evil man …'

'And we do not pray to pass by him in his hour of harvest.'

'On the path he sows thorns to hurt us in the evening …'

'His own son will run an errand in the afternoon.'

'If he lies in wait for us by the Bodiri path …'

'We will travel by the Bodiri path and not be seen by him.'

'Hmm … Mallam Nuhu!'

'Iya, *Allah Subuhana Wata'ala* will blind him,' Mallam Nuhu added, quickly.

'Hmm …'

'Ta'ala will see to it.'

Later, Mallam Nuhu aligned what Hauwa had told him about the three giants to his conjectures and impressions of what actually happened on the affected day. After he finished drinking his gruel that day, for the first time, he observed three huge men whose movements and mannerisms towards him were suspicious. One of them, except that he was younger, looked like Tambuwal. Mallam Nuhu thought he must either be his brother or some other near relation. 'Your share is with the vultures,' he swore under his breath.

While pretending not to do so, he was monitoring the movements of the three men as he prepared to leave. On his way, he met Hauwa and together they went back to the Fulani woman where he paid for her gruel. Meanwhile, the three huge men had overtaken him, apparently to waylay him ahead. Without being told, he suspected from their movements and actions towards him that such might be their plan. But he was not unduly disturbed. From his experience, *Jiba* was even more potent against human mercenaries than against other sources of molestation. Immediately after he left the village, he found an anthill and performed his ritual before proceeding. Somewhere inside the Barkada forest, he heard an uproar that sounded like men quarrelling among themselves. He smiled to himself and hummed a tune under this breath:

A man who steals from another
Despises his possessions
A man who envies another
Has lost faith in himself.

'A song with a message of truth,' Mallam Nuhu mused when he finished recollecting the events of that day. He was in the house of Gwanja where he was passing the night. The following day, he was on his way to Kahugo village.

Chapter Eight

From Kahugo to Buka Takwas

Friday, May 9th

Around 6:30 am on the 9th of May, Mallam Nuhu stood with his wares by an anthill in the outskirts of Kahugo village. He was on his way to Buka Takwas. The anthill he stood by looked like the grave of queen mother ant – an empty house whose occupants had since migrated following the death and perhaps internment of the matriarch of the house. Suddenly, a thought that had before then never occurred to him seized and possessed his mind. What if the anthill by which he stood was actually an empty shell – the grave of queen mother ant? Will his supplication before it be of any use? He was tempted to do the unprecedented – smash the anthill to confirm the presence or absence of its residents. But the temptation was soon arrested by the spiritual implications of yielding to it. If he smashes or even breaks off a part of the hill, he would have defiled the sanctity of his security with his own hands. Then, it would not matter whether the anthill was bustling with ants or was a grave. But, again, his earlier fears were valid. Communing before dead gods does no man no good. The breath wasted in such supplication was one better spared for other uses. He left the anthill in search of another. After walking and searching for an anthill for a time that was beginning to make him wonder, he saw something brownish beneath a shock of shrub leaves some metres ahead. His practised eyes immediately recognised it as an anthill. He quickened his steps. On reaching the spot, he drew the leaves of the shrub aside and peered at the anthill. Behold, it was like the one before it. Gloom seized his mind. Again, he moved off from this anthill in search of another. The third took him an even longer time to find than the second; and when he found it, it was like the first two – a seeming grave of an ants' queen mother.

'What strange afflictions have lighted on anthills in this neighbourhood?' he wondered. He was no stranger to the district he was and could remember vividly the character of the area two years ago when he last passed through the same route he was now passing through. Then, anthills, his wand of authority over men and demons were not in want in the district. 'What evil forces have taken over this land?' he thought aloud. For a land he knew to be dotted with anthills everywhere to become this vacant was like finding a desert where he knew a river to be. 'Can it be the late rains? Hardly. Ants will survive worse heat than this by migrating to the bottom of their hill where there is always less heat. Could someone had scattered the water of *fidda firutsa*, potash, salt or *bunsuru fegge* grass in this neighbourhood?'

For a moment his heart stood still then started beating violently. He had just sighted a long blade of grass that looked like *bunsuru fegge* grass. 'Who is pursuing me? What have I done?' He ran to the blade of grass, picked it up and examined it to ascertain the type of grass it was. Finding it was not the dreaded grass, his breathing became easier and his bearing clearer.

How will the wayfarer fare today unaccompanied by the security of an anthill? he wondered. If only I have my thunderbolt with me.

After a long while of standing by the anthill trying to figure out what to do, the distress in Mallam Nuhu made him attempt sitting on the anthill to think of what to do. He was in the process of unleashing his entire weight on the anthill when it crumbled crashing him and his wares into the nearby shrubs.

'Who is well?' Mallam Nuhu cried. 'I am only a roving ant … what can I do?' When he recovered himself from the crash, he went about recovering his scattered articles from near and far–flung places. All the articles were in except a pair of earrings. Mallam Nuhu was perplexed by the unity of the loss. Why not an earring of one pair with that of another? He smelled the presence of jinni around and about him. Evil conspiracy like vapours of the first rain oozed into the atmosphere. A court of superstition sprang up in his mind. A suit from the unity of the loss went and got a haughty judgment from the jury of his mystical mind. A lame sense in his haunted mind appealed to his reason, but lost the appeal to the arrogance of his superstition, which had since claimed prescience of the evil character of his experience. Evil forebodings without check sparked off fears in his mind of an attack by evil spirits. He went about tearing and bending shrubs while his eyes burrowed into every nook and cranny for the missing earrings. He did not find them. He picked the remaining articles and regained the path he left in search of an anthill. Trudging on the path, the grief of the loss of the earrings was of lesser moment to him compared to the anxiety of lack of security to see him through the great Yonaku forest that lay ahead of him. The earrings could always be acquired again. But what of his life and his remaining articles that now stood in danger of harm by human mercenaries and evil spirits? The fear of an attack by evil spirits was reinforced by the character of the missing earrings.

For a while, his fears left him when he came by two badgers known as *dage* in Hausa. These animals usually moved in twos: male and female. Mallam Nuhu was sure the twosome before him must be husband and wife. The wife was in front and the husband was behind. They were moving on the same path he was.

The badger is known to be the most jealous and easily provoked animal. If something as unseductive as a blade of grass touches the female, the male would most certainly destroy it before moving on. If a man angers the badger, it would work round to clap its teeth on the ankle of the aggressor. If it succeeds in doing so, it would not let go unless its head is severed from the rest of the body. The jealousy and ferocity of the badger has earned for it in the mouth of the Hausa man the salutation of *Dage na Halima, kyau fada a kwana ana yi*. Mallam Nuhu knew the jealousy and ferocity of the badger. So, he avoided the two badgers in front of him.

As he moved closer to River Kubura, the river beyond which laid the great Yonaku forest, he forgot about the badgers and his fears of going into Yonaku forest without securing himself, returned with a biting edge. Again, he was forced into the bush in search of the elusive anthills. By the time he regained the path, the sun had crossed to the western part of the sky. Worse, he was still an unsecured man. No anthill for his pains. However, of one thing he was now sure: he would not cross the great river and deliver himself to the great Yonaku forest without the security of an anthill. To do so would be chancing too much.

Near the bank of the river, for the third time, Mallam Nuhu branched off into the bush. This time the first thing his eyes lighted on was an anthill at the centre of a small clearing in the bush. His limbs experienced a surge of blood leaving the burden of a possible graveyard to his heart. As he drew near the anthill, he saw ants filing out of the hill in a straight line along the river.

Impulsively, Mallam Nuhu cried, 'Queen mother ant is dead! Her children had buried her and are hurrying away from her grave! Who will secure me today?'

His words fell with heavy thud on the disquieting silence of the riverside. In his distress, a flock of river birds flew over his head chirping noisily to the open country.

In the mind of Mallam Nuhu, the departing ants of the anthill represented his final break with the fortunes of that day. They marked the lowest ebb in the tide of his projections for the day. What better proof did he need that a further step forward in the present trip would cost him his life? What, if not death, is the hare who is being escorted through the country of the leopard by the tiger tarrying for when the tiger takes to his heels? He quickly retraced his steps back to Kahugo village.

Chapter Nine

Under a Neem Tree

Friday, May 9th

The night of 9th May found Mallam Nuhu under the Neem tree in front of the house of the Mai-unguwa of Kabai settlement in Kahugo village. With him were other villagers sitting on mats spread under the Neem tree. They were the usual company that came around the Mai-unguwa's court to discuss village politics lacing it with gossips. The flames of a burning bush-lamp standing some way from the company on the mats were flickering in the wind.

Sitting on the mats, meal after meal, from the homes of the men in the court maintained a steady flow to the company under the tree for the best part of an hour. The arrival of each meal was greeted by the company with 'Ahe … .he … he… ee!' As the meals arrived, so were they licked by the men under the tree. Their fingers, like the talons of crows, tore into the meals with a demented severity proper only for aggrieved vultures.

When the meals were over somebody gave a prayer, 'may God bring rain to these parts.'

'Amen!' the company answered aloud.

'These meals will not be our last.'

'And we need rain to continue to eat.'

'Is Najume still in this village?' a man to the right of Mai- unguwa asked.

'Where will he go?' another man asked. 'Where will *Mijin Hajiya* go without the permission of Hajiya?'

'I have always wondered how a man who was fathered by man can become the toy of a woman.'

'Who told you he was fathered by a man?'

'Ranka dade, Mai-unguwa; has he come to greet you since you returned from Chado?'

'Perhaps, he is still on the way.'

'But this man is an ingrate.'

'A man whose father was chased away from Akuyi by witchcraft and you Mai-unguwa received him here with open arms.'

'But who told you it was somebody's witchcraft that chased the father away? The truth is that he was the witch that was chased away because he had gone beyond devouring human beings to devouring chickens.'

'That's why when you see a man in the sun, do not hasten to bring him into the shade; find out first why he is in the sun.'

'*Asalamu alaikum,*' Najume said, making his entry into the assembly.

'*Amin alaikum salaam,*' the company chorused.

'Najume, we were just discussing Nalado your neighbour when you came in,' somebody said.

'Ah, that man …'

'*Salamu alaikum*,' another man said joining the group.

'*Wa'alaikum salaam*,' the assembly intoned.

The last man who had come was Sambo. He was best known for knowing any interesting news making its first round in the village and even beyond. The moment he sat down, he committed himself to a tale by clearing his throat. Every man shifted his buttocks. A tale was in the air.

'Mallam Nuhu, our visitor, I greet you for the second time,' Sambo said.

'Too much greeting is better than too much quarrelling,' Mallam Nuhu said.

'Mai-unguwa, I greet you for the second time,' Sambo said

'The visitor is greater than the chief of this land,' Mai-unguwa said.

'But let the visitor know there can be no guest without a host,' the company chorused.

'So, let not a fugitive from the rain start planting *kabewa* in the morning.' Mallam Nuhu said.

'In this life what do we see …?' somebody asked.

'We see a world that loves a fool but no one wants to give birth to one,' another person replied.

'The world is not a man's bedroom …' the commentary bolted into the field of general discourse on the world and the life of a man in it.

'So, let no man mistakes it for his wife.'

'It is a rented house ...'

'And we the tenants are not happy.'

'Life ...!'

'It is a joke ...'

'But nobody is laughing.'

'It is a farce ...'

'A vain man seeks to find meaning for.'

'It is a dance of little girls ...'

'Those in front fall behind and those behind fall in front.'

'As we celebrate the festival of the earth ...'

'We should be saving for the festival of heaven.'

'We have come this far...'

'Not only because he is a loving and magnanimous God, but because he has long ceased to take us serious.'

'No date is appointed for the happening of a bad thing ....'

'Only Allah knows the unknown.'

'The vulture is nobody's hen....'

'Let nobody see it as one.'

'The ways of the jinni of the air will forever remain a mystery to us humans,' Sambo gave indication of the commencement of his story.

'The man that seeks their understanding chases the wind,' someone said.

'Jinni from the Great Yonaku forest have struck again,' Sambo stepped on the threshold of his tale.

'Where? How? Many voices asked together.

'Near the bank of River Kubura on the side of Yonaku forest,' Sambo said. 'A violent dust-devil that originated from Yonaku forest blew fiercely along the path in Yonaku forest like a vengeful mad man uprooting not only trees, but carrying and slaying any human being on its path.'

An uproar of horror rose and died down.

'Imagine a wind carrying a human being.' Sambo continued. 'A thing our forefathers said could not happen has happened today. I can remember my father telling me that the wind may uproot the stoutest and largest tree and carry it away; but cannot uproot and carry the weakest and flimsiest of humans. How the Jaura man who saw the unthinkable happening today will wish my father were there to see it all with him.'

'What exactly did the Jaura man say happened?' Mai-unguwa asked.

'Ranka dade,' Sambo said slightly bowing down in reverence. 'The Jaura man said he was returning from Buka Takwas hurrying to get to the village of Shakata where he hoped to pass the night, when he heard a whizzing sound coursing through the atmosphere behind him and humming the eerie lamentation of the ghosts of Dabai.* He looked back and saw an immense dust devil whirling towards him. He leapt from the path of

---

* *A place fabled by the villagers of Kahugo village to be where ghosts held meetings characterized by eerie lamentation.*

the furious wind into the bush where he lay prostrate.

'The rat knows the cat only by the cry,' someone interjected.

'If it must tarry its eyes upon the face of the cat …'

'It will not live to remember the cry.'

'The wind ran past him like a demented horse carrying a man and a child whom it dashed against the Muno rock, killing them,' Sambo concluded his tale.

'What a terrible wind! What a harrowing death!' someone cried.

'What offence so enraged the jinni of the air to such horror?' another person wondered aloud.

'Which time did the Jaura man say this happened?' Mallam Nuhu asked.

'Between zuhur and asar,' Sambo said.

'I pray the day never comes that ants will cease being my eyes in these matters,' Mallam Nuhu prayed in his heart. To the people, he said, '*Allahu Akbar*!'

'Peace be unto His holy Prophet Mohammed,' the group chorused.

'But for the guidance of *Allah Subuhanna Wata 'ala*, I would have been caught in this whirlwind on my way to Buka Takwas today. As I journeyed near River Kubura, my mind kept telling me, "Mallam Nuhu, turn back because the road ahead runs not in your favour today." So, I heeded my mind and retraced my steps like the chameleon that smelled a raging fire before him. And now, here it is!'

'Did the Jaura man say which man and child were killed?' Mai-unguwa asked.

'No, he didn't,' Mallam Sambo said. 'All he said was that they were from the village of Sonmata half a day's trip from Halame village.'

'May Allah be merciful to the souls of all Moslems,' a man prayed.

'We are born beggars of Allah and die his beggars,' another said.

'In life, we beg for his protection, and in death we beg for his mercies,' the company concurred.

'May the day never come that he will turn deaf ears to our supplications,' a prayer went out. Then the people went on speaking as they were moved by the reported tragedy.

'We have not seen rain; we are seeing death.'

'Who is asking for human sacrifice these days to give us rain?'

'The destiny of man is a masquerade ...'

'It dances to the right; it dances to the left ...'

'No one knows its face.'

'The world is the bride of a fool ...'

'And it divorces him when it is sweetest to him.'

'A man has to handle this world with care ...'

So that it does not take him from his kinsmen and dump him in alien parts.'

'Life is a mango seed …'

'It may slip from hour hand while you are still licking it.'

'It is Mallam Nuhu, the village tradesman …'

'Nobody is sure of selling his wares and spending the money.'

'It is a debt…'

'You pay by losing that which was lent.'

'The fire that starts from the river …'

'Only Allah can quench it.'

'May this ceremony repeat itself …'

'Says a fool that has eaten the meat of a funeral ceremony.'

'We are only but roving ants, what can we do?'

'We pray to Allah to steer our paths from the path of evil.'

'Who is well?'

'Only the broken pot is well.'

'When a man is born …'

'He crawls on his knees and hands trying to gather meaning from potsherds.'

'When he thinks he has gathered enough meaning …'

'He walks about like one who knows where he came from and where he is going.'

'When he grows old …'

'Life abandons him with a stick he used to feel the depths of his disappointments.'

'Life ...'

'It is a house of mischief ...'

'Only Tagoje is amused.'

Tagoje was one of the men sitting under the neem tree. In his younger days, he was a man with abundant capacity for mischief. Even in his old age, flashes of his tendencies for mischief occasionally reminded people of who he was in his youth. Stories of his exploits in mischief were both annoying and funny.

One of such stories was when he engaged a man in a fierce fight near his farm in the bush between Kahugo and River Kubura. According to the story, the man and his wife, not known to Tagoje, as he was not known to them, were travelling from their village to another village when they met Tagoje working on his farm beside the path. After exchanging greetings with him, they continued their journey.

Four days later, the couple were returning to their village when again they came by Tagoje in his farm. The moment he sighted them, he left his hoe in the farm and ran to meet them on the path.

'Do you mean since you walked past me in this farm four days ago, you have not returned home?' he asked looking quite offended.

'Yes,' the husband replied wondering what was his interest in their time of return.

'Who do you expect to take care of your children all these days?' he demanded violently.

Before the husband could repossess his shocked wits and answer the question, Tagoje slapped him and demanded again, 'tell me who you expected to take care of your stubborn children for four long days of a single week?'

A big fight started

In another story, Tagoje while in a meeting closed his eyes, swung his head and spat. His saliva fell on the man sitting next to him. The man was angry. 'Why did you spit on me?' he demanded.

'Where do you expect me to spit?' Tagoje asked in a remorseless, provocative voice.

A fight again erupted.

In yet another story, two drunken men met him on a solitary path in a bright moonlight night and asked, 'our friend of the way, is that the moon we are seeing or is it the sun?'

'I don't know,' Tagoje said. 'I am a stranger in these parts. But you can ask the gentlemen over there,' he said, pointing at a group of sheep and goats lying nearby. 'I am sure they will know.'

The two men laughed. 'This one is more drunk than us.' They went their way and Tagoje went his way.

'Life is Tagoje ...' somebody said after a long interval of silence.

'You may be in your room and trouble will still come for you,' another finished off for him.

'It is a debt ...'

'We pay the interest now and later pay the principal.'

'It is a race ...'

'The hare is not sure of winning over the tortoise.'

'It is a song ...'

'Every man sings his tune.'

'It is a dance ...'

'We dance backward to get forward.'

'It is a glow worm ...'

'Kee nyip kee nyip.'

'It is a trick ...'

'Only Tagoje can pull it.'

'The life of a man ...'

'Is the life of the sun:

'In the morning it is weak and in the evening it is weak.'

'It emerges from darkness ...'

'And sinks into darkness.'

'We are born crying ...'

'And die crying.'

'Until a man dies ...'

'The last has not been heard from him.'

'Until death dies ...'

'Life will always be tragic.'

Chapter Ten

A Knot of Grass

There was a popular saying among *yankoli* that as a spider has various routes in the air and on the ground, so also *dankoli*. If the routes of a spider were to ensnare a prey, the routes of *dankoli* possessed enough cunning to evade any snare. So went the braggadocio of the village traders. This *chest beating*, as it is said in popular vernacular, was supported by the different means *yankoli* used to secure themselves and their wares when they went about their trade traversing rivers after wilderness and hills after streams. While some secured themselves with charms and talismans, some exploited natural forces like thunder, wind and the like.

Beside the anthill ritual, Mallam Nuhu knew other rituals of securing himself and his articles, but had always feared those alternative securities did not enjoy the same potency as that of an anthill. He had reasons for nursing such fears.

Once he tried a *knot of grass*, another form of security, but the experiment nearly cost him his life. That was in the month of July many years ago. He was traveling from the village of Kurumin Kuza to Jemage village to hawk his wares, when without looking for an anthill, he decided to try a different ritual of binding the forces of adversity in the forest. The ritual was one of weaving a knot of rooted grass to form an archway through which he would crawl after performing the ritual. After he had woven the knot of grass, he prayed:

> I am only but a grasshopper. This forest through which I will move, let all agents of evil see me as a grasshopper hopping from one blade of grass to another. Let the security of a grasshopper be my security. I hold no harm and no harm shall befall me. On the knot of these grass, I seal my security.

He removed the *laya* from his waist and laid it thrice on the knot of grass before retying it on his waist. He crawled through the archway of the knotted grass and continued his journey. By the grove of Yandoni fabled as the confluence of evil forces, a song bird chirped to a mate only for rain to start falling. It appeared to Mallam Nuhu that the rain did not extend beyond him and the grove. His skin crept and his mind went into a turmoil of misgivings. His eyes and ears became so intense in their concentration that he could see and hear the grass grow. Moving farther away from the grove, he spotted a trail of blood along the path.

'Who is well?' he whispered. He sidestepped the blood and cast its evil omen in the direction of the grove. Further down a steep slope vegetated by dense creeping plants, a huge grass snake flew at him. He screamed, 'Oh Jiba!' flung the tray containing his articles at the snake, and rolled down the slope all in a moment. The snake gave no chase but ran surly in the direction of the grove.

'… Only a roving ant and …' Before he got to Jemage village, he was shivering from high fever that made his teeth clatter. It took the combined effort of two strong medicine men to cure him of that fever.

'Knot of grass you have let the grasshopper down. It nearly lost its wings in the fire in that forest,' Mallam Nuhu protested to the persuasion that prompted his choice of that means of securing himself. 'But I thank your betrayal. I now know the shell of the tortoise and that of the snail are not the same. The tortoise itself did not know this until the day the Mayu forest caught fire.'

The Mayu forest was a hilly, thorny forest in the Darakuwa plateau. There was a popular folklore about the tortoise and the snail climbing up from a river to the top of one of the hills of the Mayu forest to graze. They were grazing on the hill when it caught fire. There was no time for any of these slow walking mollusks to get back to the river by his usual manner of walking. The only way of escaping the fire was by rolling down the slope of the hill to the marshy land of the river. The snail withdrew into his shell and rolled down to safety. The tortoise whose shell only covers his back had none to withdraw into. Nevertheless, he rolled down the slope after the snail. A sharp thorn pierced through his soft underbelly impaling him.

'How do I even know I had a shell at all?' Mallam Nuhu thought, shuddering. 'I could have just rolled down the slope with my bare flesh.' The very thought brought sweat to his forehead. 'God, how did I not get impaled on a thorn in this trip? By what stretch of good fortune did I reach the marshy land? Jiba …? Yes, I think the snake gave up chase only when I called Jiba. Hmm …Well, at least I have an opportunity the tortoise never had. I know that it is dangerous to take chances with adverse invisible means. From now on, it is either an anthill ritual or no trip for me that day.'

Chapter Eleven

Famine, Feast and Freedom

Tuesday, May 12th

The drought was still holding out against the rain like a heartless taskmaster begrudging his labourers the most petite of succour. Anxiety in the Darakuwa plateau was palpable in the air. When two villagers met, the famine in the land was there in their midst, whether or not they met in its name. They may talk about it; but often a morbid scare forbade them from talking about it. When they don't talk about it, the hush between them on the adversity in the land was more engaging of attention than talking about it.

If there was no water in the form of rainfall, there was fire in the form of heat from the sun. While drought was holding an empty bowl before the people, the flaming sun was serving panic to an already alarmed people. So intense was the heat from the sun that there was wonder among the clergy, and even not so clergy people, if hell in the sky was not leaning out to speak to people on earth.

The earth was heated to a cinder by a sun that seemed to have reached a pact with the rain to hold on while it tormented the earth for whatever iniquity. Those who could hear the air said they heard it moaning.

Anthills under Mallam Nuhu's barefoot felt like heaps of live charcoal. Sometimes, he had to cover an anthill with leaves to cool a little before venturing to place his barefoot on it. If he were not literate in ants' survival strategy of moving to the floor of their hills during hot seasons like this, he would have thought the ants had been roasted to death by this baking heat.

While the heat lasted, there was silence in the forests. The air was still and seemed to hold all things in position for the sun's proper aim. The silence in the forests was only occasionally broken by the crackling of tree branches heated to a snapping point. The occasional slight winds would not blow to relieve the baking forests. Dry leaves and other forests litters that used to rustle in the air or hop about the ground according as they were tossed or hurled by slight winds were lying lifelessly on the ground, pounded by a merciless sun. Few birds were to be seen in the fiery sky. Most birds remained in their nests and there was wonder what they were eating there. Even the lizards known for their indifference to heat were fewer and showed less agility than they were wont to.

The forests were vast cemeteries and Mallam Nuhu was the ghost that occasionally rose upon them like a bat across the surface of the moon. But even in these cemeteries, there were stirrings of muffled lives discernible only to one who shared the heartbeat of the forest.

On 12th of May, a great storm that would bring the long-awaited rain to the Darakuwa plateau came towards noon of that day. Mallam Nuhu was on his bicycle in the forest between Landa and Buka Takwas. Much of the Great Biladi forest was behind him. In the course of the night in Kahugo, he had changed his mind of moving straight from that village to Buka Takwas. Instead, he decided to go to Landa village, trade there and from there, head to Buka Takwas on his bicycle, which was in the house of Goje in Landa.

His bicycle today was in a rare spirit of performance that baffled him. It was squealing less and appeared to shuffle forward faster than before. In emitting less noise, it was at one with the still forest; in giving more speed, it was spiting defiance at the stagnant forest. Mallam Nuhu was the more surprised knowing he had not made any repairs on the old bicycle to deserve these civil manners.

Within an hour of rigorous riding, Auchan, a small hamlet between Landa and Buka Takwas was only another hour away from him at his current speed level. As he rode on, the air around him stirred in a more pressing way than before. In close succession, the rumbling of thunder and the sound of a great storm came to him whose eyes were nailed to the path of his ride. He looked back in the direction the sounds came and saw dark clouds in the east behind him. Before the clouds, a big storm was surging forward towards him.

Without stopping the bicycle, he brought down the tray containing his articles of trade from his head and placed it on the bicycle's handles where his hands were, then clamped his hands on it.

The wind revved through the mudguard of his rattletrap whipping up strings of creaking sounds that were swallowed up by the raging storm even before they got to his ears. Though he was straining hard to keep himself and the bicycle violently rocked by the storm on the path of his ride, now and then, he and the bicycle were blown off the path by the wind, but by an uncanny exertion of will he would steer himself and the bicycle back to the path again.

The wind blew long and wept deep. The sun had finally heated the air to a breaking point and it has broken. The dammed wind gushed out like water from a burst dam. There were songs of sorrow in the wind; there were songs of joy in it. Rain clouds in the east were hurled by the storm towards the west making rain unlikely only to be tossed back to the center of the sky raising hope. Mallam Nuhu before the wind didn't have to push hard on the pedals of the bicycle as he and the bicycle were hurled along by the great storm.

The rain started falling just as he was entering Auchan. It fell as if on live charcoal. None of the hissing sounds and leaping ash when water is sprinkled on fire, were missing. Each raindrop bored a muddy pit into the fevered dust of the village's trodden neighbourhood. The falling of a raindrop on the dust was like a tap on the shoulder of an edgy man. The startled dust leapt tracklessly into the air before being smothered to the ground by other raindrops. Mallam Nuhu took shelter under the eaves of a vestibule of a nearby house.

Naked children leapt into the falling rain singing and prancing about the ground. With their small, excited faces turned to the dim sky, each child was trying to claw raindrops into its open mouth and chew them under the tyranny of an unruly freedom. Now and then a blast of heavy thunder sent them scampering into near houses only to emerge again under the irresistable invitation of the pleasurable rains. Spurts of water from raindrops, like flakes of fire from the hammer and anvil of a blacksmith, flew recklessly about wetting the lower extremity of Mallam Nuhu standing under the eaves of the vestibule.

When the rain was over, he continued his journey to Buka Takwas. When he entered the forest again, it was unbelievable that things could change so sharply within the space of so fleeting a time. The forest that before the rain was a cemetery was now alive. The muffled life in it has broken out of its cocoon. Insects were shrieking and birds were chirping excitedly to each other. A herd of monkeys moved across his path gamboling and throwing their heads from side to side excited by the soothing balm of air made fresh by the rain that has just fallen. A bird recently dead, hung from the spike of a tree branch, which had impaled it. Around it, flies abandoned to the expectation of a feast were already organising themselves into a party. On the same tree, not far from where the bird hung, a chameleon stood. It was the only creature not caught by the excitement generated by the rain.

Mallam Nuhu stopped his bicycle and regarded the chameleon. Its eyes rolled forward and backward taking in all that was happening around it. There was a lot of excitement around it, but it was outside all excitement. Excitement was beneath its dignity. Excitement was a release from despair and the chameleon was beyond despair. Let the monkeys gambol and swing from tree branch to tree branch; let the birds chirp and fly madly around; let the insects shriek, the chameleon was there to observe their folly with cool detachment. It was excitement that had driven the dead bird into the spike of the tree. The chameleon was free of such monumental disaster. Let even the forest catch fire, the chameleon would not change its dignified manner of walking. Thinking of it now, Mallam Nuhu could not remember when last he came upon the dead body of a chameleon. 'Freedom from excitement helps longevity,' he said and moved on to Buka Takwas.

Chapter Twelve

An Octopus on the Road

Saturday, May 16th

In Buka Takwas, Mallam Nuhu was confronted by Hasau and Bilia two notorious armed robbers and acclaimed terrorists operating mainly in the forests between villages like Kahugo, Buka Takwas, Auchan and Kundire that fell within Mallam Nuhu's trade empire. The fear of these two armed-robbers among traders and other people traveling through the affected villages was a great one. Because traders carried more money than other travellers, they were more susceptible to attack by these vicious men of the underworld. The incessant and ruthless robbery of traders in the forests intersecting these villages made some traders treat the villages as no go areas. Not Mallam Nuhu. He traded in these villages with the same frequency and regularity he traded in other villages. Most people wondered the type of luck he had not to have fallen victim to the two dreaded robbers. Hasau and Bilia, the two armed-robbers, however appeared not to be part of that wonder. By the words of their mouths, they had attempted robbing him several times but did not succeed.

'We want to know the source of your power over us?' the two armed-robbers demanded when they confronted Mallam Nuhu in Buka Takwas.

'Who are you, and what powers are you talking about?' he asked them.

'We are Hasau and Bilia; the two armed-robbers every trader except your miserable self, dreads to hear their names,' Bilia said crowding on him.

'Well, I don't know you, and I have not even heard of these your names that are so dreaded,' Mallam Nuhu said in a stable tone that seemed to annoy the two men.

'But you know Binta my wife in Nakwana village?' Hasau asked viciously.

In spite of himself, Mallam Nuhu lost countenance. Binta ... Alhaji Nasiru's wife? God!'

'Miserable worm,' Bilia said. 'So, the horse strikes fear into you and yet the horse rider does not? You fear the lightning and not the thunder? I pity you.'

'You mean Binta, Alhaji Nasiru's wife is your…God.'

'Goat,' Bilia hissed

'The spit of a frog in a pond ...' Hasau began.

'Is like the shrieking of an insect in a madhouse,' Mallam Nuhu finished off for him. 'No one sees it; no one hears it.'

'What?'

'Listen to the shrieking of the insects.'

'Foul dog!' Hasau cried, thumping Mallam Nuhu on the chest. 'The cheeky rat in whose memory the name of the cat does not start a panic.

All these years, you have been running in and out of everywhere like the homeless rat you are, you have not heard the names of Hasau and Bilia the terrors of the forest paths … Paah …,' he spat gravely annoyed by Mallam Nuhu's denigration of their awesome standing as accomplished armed robbers and terrorists.

'Not all people know all people,' Mallam said, losing nothing of his regained composure. 'And not all people hear the names of all people. You know some; you don't get to know some. You hear the names of some people; you don't get to hear the names of some others. Knowledge and wisdom are not more than this my friends.'

'Be confident and rude as you can,' Bilia said, looking mean. 'We are inside the village surrounded by people; houses. So, the dog can taunt the hyena. A lot of liberties; take them.'

'But the hyena has the option of eating up this dog that always enters the forest; why does it submit itself to taunting in town by an effeminate dog?' Mallam Nuhu asked in that plain unemotive voice of his that courted the anger of the robbers.

'Do you think if we can finish you in the forest, we will be here talking to a worthless vermin like you?' Hasau asked, his voice bearing anger of ancient origin. 'Anytime we ambushed you in the forest when you walked or rode that your rickety bicycle past our hiding place, we saw an octopus walking on the road and even part of the forest. Not knowing where to attack, we would start quarrelling between ourselves which part of the octopus we should attack. Later, we agreed that instead of quarrelling, we should hit the head of the octopus for a trial. But strangely when you come along again, we will start quarrelling as if we never agreed on what to do. This is our frustration and anger,' he concluded.

'So, the hen should unearth the knife that will be used to slay it?' asked Mallam Nuhu with a cynical smile.

'Yes, and you must, Bilia said in a dark voice.

'The dog is telling the hyena to go back into the forest and get wisdom,' Mallam Nuhu said with a smile remotely related to his face.

'This is the sort of arrogance the bush rat exhibits until the claws of the cat teaches it the meaning of the mew, mew cry it hears in the night,' Bilia said.

'It is a poor hunter that will soon die of hunger the cat that goes hunting crying, mew, mew. For it will not find a single rat to feast on,' Mallam Nuhu said and walked hurriedly away from the armed robbers who stood looking at him in inflammable anger.

After sometimes the voice of Hasau trailed him to a nearby open mosque, 'the chameleon may pass through the fingers of the hyena like water, but soldier ants will always get him. He may melt like butter into the grass, soldier ants will sniff him out. The soldier ants here will deal with the chameleon over there!'

Mallam Nuhu's heart leapt down. He could not reply to the grim threat. The one creature the chameleon cannot evade is the soldier ant. That is why the chameleon does not come out whenever soldier ants are abroad.

'The bush is still burning,' Bilia's voice followed that of Hasau while Mallam Nuhu was still under the fear of Hasau's threat. 'So, the grasshopper should not congratulate itself yet!'

'Tell that to the tortoise!' Mallam Nuhu shouted back in good humour. 'It is a snail in that forest, not a grasshopper.'

'We will burst the shell of the snail!' Bilia replied Mallam Nuhu. 'If we can't find where to pierce it, we will roast the damn thing. I surely will kill the itinerant ant. I will use potash to cook it and salt to eat it with!' Together, the two armed-robbers slung away their anger hissing poison.

On hearing this last threat, Mallam Nuhu felt weak at the knees. He could no longer stand. Clutching the wall of the mosque, he put his wares on the ground and sat down on a block beside the mosque. His heart was thumping wildly. 'They would chase away the ants with salt and potash. Was it not what they said? Terrible!' His teeth were on edge and there were little pools of perspirations on his forehead. A great need to relieve his bowels took hold of him who often went for days without defecating, but who now had to excrete for the second time in a day still very much in its youth. There was a vast vacant land behind the mosque. He ran into the land and squatted behind a *chediya* tree. 'If they can chase away the ants from the forest with salt and potash, they would have cracked the shell of the snail,' he thought while squatting behind the tree. 'Could these crooks have taken potash and salt to the forest between Kahugo and Buka Takwas?' he wondered. 'No, they can't afford to waste their money on potash and salt. Perhaps, it was the water of *fidda firutsa* and *bunsuru fegge* grass that they used. These would cost them nothing. But I can't remember seeing traces of any of these purgatives in that forest ... The world can only come to sorrow with evil people like you,' he said and spat out saliva that felt bitter in his mouth. For days, he was sick and could not go trading.

In Buka Takwas, Hasau and Bilia were laughing and thumping each other.

'So, it is true this man thinks he has magical powers that makes him appear like an octopus in the forest,' Hasau said.

'Imagine!' returned Bilia, laughing. 'If he believes, he is an octopus, why does he keep changing paths to avoid us?'

'He is indeed a funny man,' Bilia said. 'But we have done very well for ourselves today. If formerly he had any doubt he is an octopus in the forest, he will now believe he is one. It is such confidence that will betray him into our hands.'

Chapter Thirteen

Out in the Rain

Friday, July 3rd

Yaddakunni and Malmala villages fell within the litany of villages Mallam Nuhu took his wares to. The path between the two villages was intersected by three rivers and four streams. The rivers had raft bridges while the streams had none. In the peak of the rainy season, the raft-bridges were often overflowed by floods. When this happened, it was always difficult even for a raft man to fathom the depth of a buried bridge.

On 3rd of July, Mallam Nuhu resumed his trade. He had fully recovered from his sickness. He set out with his wares from Yaddakunni village to Malmala village a refreshed man out to battle all obstacles that stood between him and his trade. Very little rain fell the previous night in Yaddakunni village where he passed the night and so he assumed he would not have problem with a river on account of a flood. He was right with regard to River Gamau, the first river across the path to Malmala. But he was wrong with regard to River Pankam. This river was gurgling with flood when he got to it. This night rain was not ubiquitous as the common saying goes about night rain. It was rather uneven in its distribution,

He had journeyed so far from Yaddakunni village that going back was unreasonable. To wait on the riverbank for the flood to subside, he might have to wait the whole day because River Pankam, before which he stood, was not a sandy river that absorbed water fast, but a clay bedded river that took its time in such process even at the beginning of the rainy season when the earth was thirsty for water. To compound his predicament, lowering clouds were brimming up in the eastern skies for the proverbial heavy rainfall that was said to prevent ants from fetching fire from their neighbours.

Mallam Nuhu picked a nearby stick and struck the watercourse where he knew the raft bridge was. The stick was rapidly seized by swift water current and floated downstream. Placing the tray containing his merchandise a little into the bush, he applied himself to severing a bamboo stick from a stock near the blind path he moved on. After twisting and jerking for some time, the stick came off. He tore off the leaves and wrung off the reedy part of the stick to produce a sturdy stick. Holding the stick with both hands, he again struck the water to locate and determine the depth of the bridge under the water. The stick encountered no bridge.

The bridge had been washed away. With dark clouds overhead, his chances were fast dissolving into a sinister mess. Though he could swim, the water current appeared too strong, particularly that he had to carry his articles with him. Apart from the physical inconvenience of swimming across the river with his wares, if he could manage to do so, there was the fear that the *garlic* he was carrying amongst other articles could cause his death in the hands of water spirits known as *yan ruwa* by yankoli. Garlic was known among yankoli to attract mermaids and other water spirits so much that whoever had it on him and made the mistake of wading into any big water body, water spirits would claim him along with the garlic. He was still wondering what to do, when the clouds burst.

The fear of thunder would not allow Mallam Nuhu to take shelter under a tree. He could not remember the number of men thunder had killed while taking shelter from rain under trees. About five years ago, Shuaibu, his childhood friend, was returning from the farm with his son when they were overtaken by heavy rainfall. While the son continued with his homeward journey, Shuaibu went to take shelter under a locust beans tree by the roadside. He had barely finished finding a good position to shelter himself under the tree when thunder struck blowing him to pieces. A year ago, it was Danasabe that was killed by thunder while sheltering under a mango tree in his guinea corn farm. To Mallam Nuhu, thunder was a hunter and trees were the games it hunted. It was therefore flirtation with death to stand by this game while the hunter was on the prowl.

There was a popular belief that a man struck to death by lightning went straight to paradise. 'Well, well! Such will certainly be strange,' Mallam Nuhu murmured musing over the belief. 'Hunters do not take their games to paradise, wherever paradise is, after killing them. The fly caught in the cobweb of the spider we all know what happens to it.'

If only I have my thunderbolt with me, I would have taken shelter under any of these trees, he thought bitterly. Without it… I am a tortoise in Mayu forest. Hmm … Here I squat with my body shielding my wares … Without the rain stone, my thunderproof cape, I can be surer of holding this mango seed here than under any of these trees,' he murmured. 'This mango seed may be bitter … but … but who knows the taste of the seed beyond?'

The rain went on pouring for more than an hour before petering into drizzles. Throughout this time, Mallam Nuhu kept shifting ground as the flood kept swelling, annexing new territories hitherto beyond its reach. Whenever he squatted, he hovered over his merchandise like a hen over her chicks. Later, the drizzles fizzled out leaving a sodden earth and atmosphere in its wake. Mallam Nuhu stood up and stared at the sea before him. The frontiers of his hope against such an assaulting sight were clearly defined by the frailty of his means and the burden of his wares. For a moment he considered going back to Yaddakunni village. However, the thought was soon chased away by the possibility of a flood in River Gamau behind him, following the recent heavy rainfall. His mind returned to the challenge of River Pankam before which he stood. The thought of how long he would have to wait for the river to subside to a crossing level alarmed his distressed mind. His anxiety was compounded by his knowledge of River Nakurna beyond River Pankam before which he stood. For that river might spring an unpleasant surprise of its own like river Pankam when he gets to it. Thus, behind him was a hyena and in front of him was a wolf, as a goat might mourn its predicament.

How well I would have been if I were a spider, he thought. How sweet it would have been to spring across this vast sea on a bridge of my saliva? No, no, how well I would have been if I were a bird that needs no bridge to get to the other side of this great mess? As he thought, a giant eagle swooped down the river as if to land on the water only to rebound, flapping its wings loudly as it sailed through the air to the other side of the river.

'God who made me!' Mallam Nuhu exclaimed. 'God who made me! I am too heavy for the air so I have to wait for that which can carry my weight. Who is well?'

He squatted down to wait for the subsidence of the flood in River Pankam whenever that would be. Whatever lay in stock for him in River Nakurna, he would take when he gets to that river. The consolation for this decision was that it was carrying him forward in his journey and not backward.

Towards evening, a man about his age came by. This man was walking listlessly down the river without the air of a destination. On his back was a shop of rags into which big bushflies flew and came out with things Mallam Nuhu could not see. Though walking clear of the flood, the man appeared to Mallam Nuhu to be floating on the water with other odds and pieces of wood carried by the flood downstream. He walked past Mallam Nuhu without even turning to look at him. He seemed even scarcely aware of the flood Mallam Nuhu thought he was floating on. In every way, he looked like a man life had locked out and was contented to remain outside without even a knock on the door. He was a man sufficiently offended by life that he was incapable of taking any offence against his violator. Mallam Nuhu's gaze fled from him back to the flood.

By sunset, the flood was yet to subside to a level safe for him to attempt crossing the river. He became more anxious. The village of Malmala, which he was going to, was still very far from where he stood and that of Yaddakunni which he had left was even farther. Moments later, he saw a Fulani man with his cattle approaching; then, he saw two lads running out of the herd to bring four straying cows into the fold. Excitement and sorrow mingled in Mallam Nuhu's heart.

When the Fulani man came closer to where he was, Mallam Nuhu saluted him, *'Barka da warhaka Agwai.'*

The Fulani man answered, *'yauwa* Mallam Nuhu, *barka da yamma.'*

Although Mallam Nuhu knew he was known in all villages within his trade empire, he didn't know his fame had gone beyond settled villagers to nomadic herdsmen. He was therefore shocked to hear a Fulani nomad he had never seen before calling his name with such familiarity.

'Where do you know me?' he asked the Fulani man not hiding his surprise.

'Ah ah, Mallam Nuhu, who does not know you in these parts. The popularity of your trade has spread your name through the villages and the bush like a wild fire in the moon of *Jumadah Awwal.* I think even the forests and rivers know you.'

'Nmm ...' Mallam Nuhu grunted. 'Please, *Agwai* that knows Mallam Nuhu but whom Mallam Nuhu does not know, can you by any means assist Mallam Nuhu cross this river? He has been waiting since afternoon for the flood to subside and he is going to Malmala village,' he entreated the Fulani man without knowing in which way he could be of help in the circumstance.

'This river has a lazy appetite even when hungry,' the Fulani man said. 'It sips water like the *genka* bird. Waiting for it to subside is like waiting for a tortoise to climb down Jangir Mountain. Now that it rolls in satiation, it may even be vomiting water to welcome you instead of absorbing it to allow you to pass.'

'That will not be fair,' Mallam Nuhu permitted himself a searing amusement. 'More so, that it knows me.'

'The distress of a guest is the peculiar desire of an absurd reception,' the Fulani man said. 'I don't want you to quarrel with your patience by this river. Follow me to my kraal and sleep over this flood. A river that enjoys a grotesque welcome deserves not the presence of its guest,' the Fulani man said in a flush of comic banter.

'Thank you,' Mallam Nuhu said, his face gaining in amiability. 'Truly, the traveller's home is everywhere.' He carried his wares to his head and followed the Fulani man. 'By the way, you have not told me where and how you knew me,' he said on their way to the kraal.

'Where I knew you? Everywhere. You are a nomad and I am a nomad and nomads are everywhere. I knew you everywhere,' the Fulani man said grinning. 'How I knew you? Ha ha ha! The flies that follow a nomad tell him a lot of things. The cattle egrets that follow the herd of a shepherd sometimes fly up to spy yonder lands for him. They bring names of other sojourners on the land,' the Fulani man said in playful mischief.

Tears came to the eyes of Mallam Nuhu. Poor cattle egret sowing without reaping, he thought, mournfully. The story was a popular one amongst Fulani herdsmen that cattle egrets follow cows hoping that the eyes of the cows would be falling out of their sockets for them to feed on. 'True, all nomads know themselves,' he said touched by the Fulani man's blend of humour and mischief. 'I am a nomad; yet I don't know my fellow nomad.'

'Are you sure you don't know me?'

'As sure as I am of the flood in River Pankam.'

'Are you still sure?' the Fulani man asked, taking off his pasturing hat and turning to face Mallam Nuhu with an infectious smile.

'Jonga Ardo!' Mallam Nuhu cried. 'I should have guessed from your musical voice,' he more or less reproached himself for his failure of recollection. 'Jonga Ardo, the flute man of the forest; the solitary kite that perches on a blade of grass!'

'All nomads know themselves,' Jonga Ardo said

'Yes,' replied Mallam Nuhu in deep agreement. About six years ago, he first met Jonga Ardo sitting alone on a rock inside river Takwano. He was playing a melodious tune on his flute to the lonely river and the forest beyond. The mesmerizing tune from his flute so melodiously wove into the clasp and yawn of the river and forest that he could see the boughs and leaves of trees swaying in tune with the melody from Jonga's flute. His eyes grew misty with tears as he stood listening to Jonga Ardo's music that engaged nature in a celebration of life. He stood quietly where he was willing Jonga to play on, never to stop until all creation melt into a wax of happiness in an ecstasy of a rapture that celebrates the end of life. Such was his involvement in Jonga,s music that he outstripped Jonga's participation in the music. So, when Jonga abruptly stopped the music, he who had overshot himself was left still very much inside the music that captured and possessed his being.

'Ah, Modibo, who are you?' Jonga had asked bringing him back to earth.

'Mallam Nuhu,' he answered, mechanically.

'I am Jonga Ardo the flute man of the forest; the solitary kite that perches on a blade of grass. Where are you coming from?'

'I am coming from everywhere and I am going everywhere.'

'Are you the wind?'

'No, no, no. I am dankoli a tradesman that has no address. What are you doing here playing such a soulful tune with no one but the trees to sway to?'

'When I can, I play for the forest, for the birds and the monkeys. I am the forest flute man, remember.'

'Yes, I will always remember the forest flute man and the solitary kite that perches on a blade of grass,' he said and meant it. 'Playing for the trees, the birds and the monkeys does not earn you a living, what do you do for a living?'

'Although my pasturing hat and stick are not here, you should know I am a Fulani herdsman.'

'I guessed so, but wanted confirmation.'

'You now have it.'

'Where are your articles of trade? I am here with mine.'

'My cattle are with my children. I observe days of rest. Today is one of such days. When I play for Allah's creation, my flute is a sufficient companion. When the birds sing for me, they do not peck for food at the same time,' Jonga said and laughed.

'A likeable man you are,' he had said and waved goodbye to Jonga Ardo who soon commenced his music again. He had pinned his ears to the sound of Jonga's music, to its echo and to its memory as he moved farther and farther away from Jonga Ardo.

He never forgot Jonga Ardo, and as it turned out, Jonga did not forget him either. Each had left his presence in the mind of the other like the footprint of Takina in Banya swamp.* His delayed recognition of Jonga was partly because of the pasturing hat he had never seen on him before; and partly because of his distress.

In popular Hausa folklore, Takina was a giant from the east who marched through Banya a long stretch of swamp in the Darakuwa plateau leaving giant footprints that were still visible to sojourners of the Banya swamp.

Am I the wind? How I wish I am the wind, he thought, returning from his journey into the past. As the wind, you wouldn't have found me waiting before this fright. 'Life ...'

'It is an unkind tax collector,' Jonga Ardo finished off for him.

'It smiles at a fool ...'

'And he thinks it is wooing him. Everybody, get ready for a wedding feast,' he would cry. Mmm ... How lucky the world is to have a fellow like him.'

'It smiles at a wise man ...'

'And he warns himself: "man, take care; a wolf is smiling at you."

'It is a bee...'

'He who will take the honey must not complain of the stings.'

'Jonga Ardo,' Mallam Nuhu saluted. 'On which blade of grass is the kite perching tonight?'

'We are near it,' Jonga said and shouted an order in Fulfulde to his children to bring some cows that were straying into a guinea corn farm. It turned out the intervention of his children was unnecessary as the cows seemed to have heard his command; for on their own, they turned back and headed into the fold once more.

'Without doubt, if a cow will hear and speak any language, it will be that of the Fulani herdsman,' Mallam Nuhu thought.

As the sun was slipping into the western horizon where it was interned for the night, a long column of smoke that shot into the horizon told Mallam Nuhu they were near Jonga's kraal. The lowing noise of calves welcoming their mothers home soon took over the atmosphere. The smell of cow dung rose in a stable unity and tailed the noise.

When they climbed up a small hill, the kraal came into their view as they came into its view also. Calves that were not taken to pasture raced from the stable ground near the camp lowing welcome to their mothers and the mothers lowed back in reply. As soon as a calf got to its mother, it slid under the mother's stomach and with one violent push start sucking its udders hungrily. The mother on its part would momentarily halt its homeward journey for its calf to do some sucking before they both moved on to the stable. Often, for a cow and its calf to move on, either Jonga or any of his children would have to wield their pasturing sticks. The expert manner the herdsmen wielded their sticks against their cattle never failed to impress Mallam Nuhu. Whether it was Jonga or any of his children that was wielding his stick, the expertise was the same: colourful. The stick rolled in the air with a faint whizzing sound, perhaps to warn the offending cattle of an impending reprimand before the stick fell on it. He observed that as the stick moved closer to the cow, it became suspended in the hand of the wielder and ended up whacking than beating the cattle. The cattle having received the warning of the whizzing sound was obliged to move on, more by reciprocity than by any force.

They arrived the ground that served as the stable for Jonga's cattle before getting to the camp inhabited by Jonga and his family. The stable was marked off by a pale of wooden stems driven into the ground and connected to each other for firmness by ropes made of raffia. The gates provided access into the pale and exit out of it. They were only opened to let in cattle or let them out.

Small heaps of camwood and cow dung were smouldering generating more smoke than any fire a casual observer might think they were supposed to generate. But to a Fulani herdsman familiar with the process, that was how they were supposed to burn. If they generate more fire, they will soon burn out exposing the cattle to excessive cold for the rest of the night. But if a little, they would burn throughout the night and thus keep the cattle warm for the whole night. Mallam Nuhu waited for Jonga and his children to secure the cows to small pegs that dotted the stable before they all moved into the kraal.

Like the stable, the kraal stirred when they came in. Women left their cooking pots on fire in small hearths to welcome them by curtsying several times on the ground while repeating phrases like *ayanli jam, ahirti jam* which means good evening in Fulfulde language. They repeated the greeting as many times as they curtsied. Much of their greeting was directed at Mallam Nuhu the stranger.

After the evening meals that came in different calabashes, he was taken to the hut he was to pass the night. The bed he was to sleep on was a row of small stems of wood arranged together in the form of a platform and covered with a mat of raffia. Mallam Nuhu slept on this bed as soundly as a king would on a royal bed.

For the next one week, he stayed with Jonga Ardo in his kraal. In the daytime, he went to trade in several other Fulani kraals near and far from Jonga's kraal. At sunset, he repaired to Jonga's kraal for the night. Twice, he followed Jonga to River Takwano when the latter went to play soulful tunes on his flute. From Jonga's kraal, he proceeded to Baucha village in the eastern part of the Darakuwa plateau.

Chapter Fourteen

The Inhospitable Host

Monday, August 3rd

Baucha was a very big village surrounded by a host of several small villages. Mallam Nuhu spent three weeks in this village. Each day, he went to trade in different parts of the village or in a neighbouring village returning to Baucha in the night. From Baucha he went to Jita. From Jita, he set out for Malmala.

The road between Jita and Malmala village was a long winding road that kept a traveller on it perpetually on the wings of sudden appearances of other people moving on the road. Mallam Nuhu was on his way from Jita village where he passed the previous night to Malmala village where he was taking his trade. This moment, he was wondering if ever God would avenge him against Tambuwal who had appropriated his thunderbolt, the next moment he was thinking of what prospects lay in Malmala village for his trade, the other moment he had thought of the inhospitable attitude of the *Mai-unguwa* of Jita village in whose house he passed the previous night.

The *Mai-unguwa* whose house he used to pass the night whenever he was in Jita had died and a new one had been appointed in his place. This new one he neither knew his person nor his house. The new *Mai-unguwa* also did not know Joseph.* He had arrived the village at a time all, except households in the habit of late cooking, had finished their meals and elderly people were retiring to bed. It was one of those bright moonlit nights that a keen eye in the countryside could spot a roving ant on the ground. It was the sort of moonlight that was said to escort a fool to the forest to be hanged by evil spirits. It was the sort of night that invited children out for moonlight tales and various village sports. In Jita village, while some children gambolled on the paths that connected the various quarters of the village, others were playing in various forecourts before various compounds and also in the village square. He approached a group of children playing in the village square, greeted them and asked of the house of the new *Mai-unguwa* of the village.

A little girl said he was asking of her house because she was the daughter of the *Mai-unguwa*. She led him to the house. The *Mai-unguwa* was not happy with his coming though he later tried to hide his displeasure in a facade of hospitality.

From where he stood at the entrance of the house waiting to be invited in, he could hear the *Mai-unguwa* scolding the girl and rapping his knuckles on her head for foolishly bringing unknown and uninvited guests to his house. Who

---

* *After the death of Joseph in Egypt a new pharaoh who did not know Joseph came to power and started maltreating the Israelites Exodus 1:8*

told her he was a *Gamji* tree under whose shade all may take shelter? he asked her again and again while thrashing her with a small cane. The girl went on crying long after he had stopped beating her.

He at the entrance of the house felt sorry for the girl, but there was nothing he could do. Leaving the house in search of alternative accommodation would have been the least he could do for her. But he could not see the feasibility of such alternative accommodation. Lest in pity for the girl, who in any case, had already received her punishment, he stirs a fresh strife in another house. He hung by the gate repeating *assalamu alaikum* at reasonable intervals.

Usually, *assalamu alaikum* is a salutation of peace and goodwill. From Mallam Nuhu standing at the entrance of the house, *assalamu alaikum* was said loudly to warn jinni standing on the doorway to move out of the way; otherwise, he might step over them and bring about his death. His fifth *assalamu alaikum* produced the *Mai-unguwa* at the gate. *'Amin alaikum salaam wa rahamatullah,'* he said in such a hypocritical, cheerful voice that had he not heard him beating and scolding the little girl, he would have thought what a cheerful, hospitable man.

The Mai-unguwa ushered him in with such frivolous hospitality that made him wonder why a man should be cowardly towards another in his own house. For to cowardice he attributed the *Mai-unguwa's* hypocritical show of hospitality.

After they shook hands, he introduced himself and why he was in the house. When the former *Mai-unguwa* was alive, he used to stay the night in his house whenever he was in the village. Now that he was dead, the house of the new *Mai-unguwa* automatically suggested itself to him as his new guest-house.

'You are welcome to my house anytime, Mallam Nuhu dankoli,' the *Mai-unguwa* said.

'Thank you very much,' he said. However, both men understood each other. He was not welcome in the *Mai-unguwa's* house any time.
'It is unfortunate you arrived when we have just finished our dinner,' the *Mai-unguwa* said again.

'Don't worry,' he said.

Again, both men understood each other. Both knew the *Mai-unguwa's* house had finished no dinner. The little girl who brought him to the house had told him on their way to the house that *tuwon masara* was being prepared by her mother. She had told him in the innocent manner children tell visitors to their house what they had eaten or was being cooked in the house. What the little girl told him soon acquired an embarrassing authority when a little girl that looked like the one that brought him to the house walked past them in the vestibule holding a covered calabash that apparently contained food being taken to a neighbour. Whatever doubt he would have still entertained was put to rest by *Mai-unguwa's* frantic attempt to douse his suspicion. As soon as the girl moved into the vestibule on her way out of the house, *Mai-unguwa* abruptly started a conversation that was strange and isolated between people who were meeting for the first time.

'You know, I used to be a wealthy man with forty goats, eight cows and twenty sheep. That was when I was living in Dankundi village before I migrated to this village,' he began.

In his mind, he said, 'is your present penury the reason for your miserliness?' To *Mai-unguwa* he said in a voice laced with cynicism, 'even now I don't know how many of these cattle you still have.'

From the way *Mai Unguwa* continued his story without any form of embarrassment, it was clear that either he did not spot the cynicism in Mallam Nuhu's voice or he did, but was a liar who knew no shame on being found out.

'As I said, I was living in Dankundi not far from this village,' he continued in a stable voice clear of any shame. 'About *25* years ago in Dankundi, cattle thieves broke into my stable one night taking away all my cattle, but two cows and four sheep. Robbers' invasion of cattle stables in the village became so incessant and heartless that most households in the village were forced to flee to this village and other parts. My family is one of such households. In fact, most of the inhabitants of this quarter of Jita village are refugees of the

robbers' invasion of Dankundi village,' he concluded himself half believing his false story.
'Really?' he had grunted. He could not bring himself to say anything to a bunch of lies told with such calm and conscienceless piety. His anger was how a cheap liar and hypocritical man like the one before him could be made a *Mai-unguwa* to lead others and settle their disputes. Well, that was the headache of his subjects that made him chief over them. Sleep time came and he was told the cow skin he sat on in the vestibule would be his bed for the night. He thanked the *Mai-unguwa* for his *hospitality* and lay down to sleep. Soon, the *Mai-unguwa,* his cheap lies and hypocrisy were lost in a land of rolling forests, falling clouds and floating rivers.

'Gee ... gee ... Mall.am Nuhu, you are welcome.'

'Juu. . .juu. . . Mallam Nuhu, you are welcome.'

Honey bears and squirrels leapt at him joyously in this strange land of pleasing manners. To each he was giving a piece of his wares saying, 'you are a friend and I don't sell to mannerly friends like you.'

The following morning, he left the *Mai-unguwa*'s house within that space of dawn in which night the rolling sheet of death takes a final flight from the advancing army of day whose war drums had woken frogs and woodpeckers to a celebration of the memories of life.

Entering the forest, he found he was happier than he was in Jita village. 'But I can't sell to animals. I can only sell to human beings and they live in villages … Mai-unguwa, Mai-unguwa! Hmm …'

Chapter Fifteen

Two Tradesmen met on a Road

Monday, August 3rd

Thinking and talking about *Mai-unguwa* Mallam Nuhu suddenly came upon Sidi, a very close acquaintance of his, who was coming from Malmala to Jita village.

Sidi was a tall middle-aged man whom poverty and toil had impoverished to old age ahead of his time. Once he had a dislocation on his right leg that infected his movement with a noticeable limp. The dislocation had since healed but the limp had refused to go with the dislocation that brought it. It had become one of those deformities a man carries to his grave. He let it be. The task of earning a living was engaging enough without the distraction of such vanity as the regularity of his corporal motion. He was beyond the cares of regard others had of him.

Sidi was in the trade *of jaura,* which perhaps was more nomadic than the dankoli trade of Mallam Nuhu. The trade of *jaura* essentially consisted of hawking soup items like *kuka, kubewa, borkono* and *dadawa.* 'Tiger of the forest!' Sidi hailed Mallam Nuhu.

'Jaura jikan Jaura!' Mallam Nuhu saluted back.

'You who know all the ant paths of the forests!' Sidi continued his salutations. 'The footprints of the elephant that cover those of the camel! The mighty boar that swallows the python! Elephant, the moving hut of the forest! The flying bat that has seen all nights! You to whom returning home is a shame. The leopard is wandering and the tiger is wandering. One day, they will meet. My brother, I greet you.'

'*Jaura Jikan Jaura!*' Mallam Nuhu saluted Sidi again. 'The great one who knows all the trees of the forests and their ancestry! The man whose pursuit of wealth raises a whirlwind! You to whom returning home is a scandal! The lazy man sells his land to buy gruel and says it is better; you sell your articles to buy land and say it is better. If a man's wealth were commensurate with his strife, you should be in the air on board your plane and I should be on the road on board my car!'

'Even more than that,' Sidi said.

'Let's get the weight off our legs,' Mallam Nuhu said going to sit under the shade of a tree beside the path. '*Jaura,* our strifes are mightier than our wealth,' he continued reclining his back against the tree. 'The roving water jar is often empty while the mighty water pot at home is often full.'

'Such is life,' Sidi said.

'The back of the farmer receives the sun and the rain while his stomach gathers the fat. The man in the shade is often fatter than the man in the sun.'

'Why then do you and I bother?' Sidi said joining Mallam Nuhu under the shade.

Mallam Nuhu's heart skipped a beat. Beneath his calm composure had recently lurked the query, 'why carry on when it is apparent that hot pursuit of wealth does not bring it. Why not go to the shade and take your chance with vultures feasting on providence? Why not curry favour with the mad truth?' These thoughts of frustration with the fortunes of his trade often came upon him in moments of despair when it appeared he laboured to too miserly a harvest. People had praised his dogged struggle to achieve prosperity in his trade, but he alone knew his anxiety and fears of failure. Now the question by Sidi again stoked the doubt that undermined his faith in industry. 'A man does not cry in public,' he said to himself in his effort to conceal his feelings. 'If a man must remain a man, he must not remove his trousers and wear wrappers.' To Sidi, he said, 'because we know fortune does not marry the sluggard for long. Sooner or later, she deserts him to roam the paths looking for a worthy husband.'

'*Allahu Akbar!* Sidi ululated. 'I have always envied your spirit that does not know the pains of despair. You are a lucky man to be in life and not know care. Please, pray it is miserable people like me the mistress of fortune crosses their path soon, because you need her less.'

How selfish people can be, Mallam Nuhu thought. To desire the shadow of the moving clouds over your head while not caring how I benefit from the same fortune of heaven, shows a heart that wonders why a particular misfortune should befall it and not someone else. To Sidi, he said, 'my brother of the paths, the leopard is wandering and the tiger is wandering; one day they will meet. Remember?'

'Now, you are talking again.'

'I know the day is not far when the path of one of us will meet with that of fortune. Then she will say to whoever it is, come and claim me my husband. Then only he will hear her voice because only he has learned to hear the trees when they talk, the grasses when they laugh and the rivers when they weep. Only he sees the birds when they beckon and the shrubs when they sigh.'

'The language of the forest is for the forest people.'

'If a fish cannot hear the river, it will die in the morning of its birth.'

'And be buried by the path of the water snake.'

'The water snake shall make his nest over that grave.'

'Its poison shall be libation for that fish.'

'We walk like the tortoise, but shall reach where we are going before the hare gets to where he is going,' Mallam Nuhu said and laughed.

'I envy you,' Sidi said without a rise in his humour.

'Why should you envy me?'

'You care for nothing and you have two bicycles. I still don't have a pedal.'

This man does not know that envy is a lake of fire that burns itself out and becomes ashes if it cannot find anything to burn, Mallam Nuhu thought. He does not know that the ashes of envy are the manure that fertilizes the gardens of the person envied. 'Fortune comes in rags ...' he said.

'Some men take it for a pauper,' Sidi finished off for him.

'Others take it for a mad man and deny it a handshake.'

'But wise men see it as the mad truth.'

'The mad truth?' Mallam Nuhu asked of no one.

'Yes, the mad truth and they shake hands with it.'

'The mad truth ...'

'Surely, the mad truth.'

'It is the child that raises his hands ...'

'That the father picks up.'

'And gives a plum of *kulikuli* to.'

'Which river will I take her to drink water ...'

'Says a lazy, poor man that has purchased a hen.'

'But even the journey to the river, his legs will say someone is using them.'

'We will not labour like the cattle egret which knows no rest in its wandering life ...'

'Going after cattle in the vain hope of feeding on the eyes of the cows ...'

'Only to die without pecking the eye of a cow.'

'My knowledge of our way forbids me to ask where to this morning,' Sidi said embracing Mallam Nuhu.

'Why should one cow ask the other the meaning of chewing the cud?' Mallam Nuhu said. 'The herdsman goes rearing his cattle and the farmer goes tilling his land without inquiry. They understand each other.'

'What have the ants taught you today?'

'That a man should be industrious before being greedy,' Mallam Nuhu answered. 'That a glutton is their cow. He milks himself and others only for them to milk him. What have they taught you?'

'That if all men work day and night, there will be no time for envy and gossips,' Sidi answered.

'Let's continue to save when we can the cents we have been saving in our little holes. One day, they will make a fortune. Let's continue to spend our poverty on the paths to get the riches we desire. God is not an oppressor.'

'I hope so.'

'Sidi!'

'Yes?'

'Sidi.'

'Surely, surely, he is not.'

'Good; if we lose our *iman,* we lose the right path and if we lose the right path, we go astray into the path of *iblis* the evil one.'

'Sure. We are men of the paths. We know that a man who loses the right path will not get to the next village where he hopes to make a lot of sales. Such a man will most certainly stray into the vultures and hyenas of the evil one.'

'God help us.'

'Amin summa amin.'

'If there is a bastard in any house we passed the night, may he not be the first person we set our eyes on waking up in the morning.'

'Amin summa amin!'

The belief was common that if there is a bastard in a house, he should not be the first person one would set his eyes on in the morning. If, he was the first person one sighted in the morning, all kinds of misfortune would befall the person so unlucky. If he was a trader, he would not sell his wares that day.

'Should you return first to this path, leave a sign by this spot to tell me you returned in peace,' Mallam Nuhu said disengaging from Sidi.

'Do the same for me,' Sidi said.

The two men moved off with the understanding that whoever first returned to the point of their separation, would indicate his return by leaving a bundle of leaves or some other sign beside the path informing the other of his earlier return.

About thirty metres apart, Mallam Nuhu looked back at the tree they had just rested under and cried, 'Yii Sidi! we have just rested under a baobab tree in this hot afternoon. Yii!'

Particularly amongst village tradesmen, the belief was very strong that standing under a baobab tree at mid-day brings about madness.
Sidi, without betraying alarm or shock at Mallam Nuhu's discovery, gradually turned round and beheld the tree they had just left. 'No wonder!' he said with a strange glee Mallam Nuhu had never seen on anybody's face before. 'Does it really matter? Perhaps madness may cure me of my various ailments. My brother of the paths!' he shouted at Mallam Nuhu, 'may you not sell all your articles in this trip!' Again, he bid farewell to Mallam Nuhu and turned on his way.

Mallam Nuhu waved back smiling wanly at him. For a fleeting moment, there was something like fear on his face; but it was soon replaced by an expression of shock and dismay. He shook his head and stared fixedly at the retreating form of Sidi without uttering a word. Finally, he cried, 'however, whatever!' He turned and scampered away. 'Hmm ... Binta ... And you, baobab tree. Thank God, I sat with the ants under your shade while he stood in the wind which has apparently entered his head. Ah!' he cried and quickened his steps towards Malmala village. '... Sarkin Noma, Jiba will avenge me.'

Chapter Sixteen

A Night out in the Forest

Wednesday, August 5th

Over the years that Mallan Nuhu had been in the business of dankoli, he had come to accept erratic fluctuation of sales as a permanent feature of the trade. One day, he might make sales of more than two pounds. In another, he might make sales less than two shillings or even one shilling. But, never was there a day he went about his trade without making a single sale. That day came in Malmala where he went after leaving Jita village. Several times he was called or beckoned to by women interested in his wares, all these times nothing was bought by any of the women. By evening, he had walked round the entire village house by house without a single article being purchased. He became restless.

'When did I set my eyes on a one-eyed man today?' he racked his brains to recall if he had met a one-eyed man early in the morning that day, but could not recall such encounter. Like other rural folks of his time, he believed that if a person comes across a one-eyed man early in the morning before washing his face, he would not make or receive money from any source that day.

'No point for a bird remaining perched on a tree that has no fruit,' he said, pulling his nose in a thoughtful manner that denoted he was taking a decision. He carried his merchandise and hurried out of the village.

The next village was Wakiluwa, a far village to make by trekking. But Mallam Nuhu heeding only one voice: 'Get yourself and your articles as far as your feet can take you from the land of Chabiya* took off from Malmala village to Wakiluwa village in the evening.

At the outskirts of the village, he saw the blade of a hoe lying in a little clearing in the bush. He moved near it and found it had been perforated. Using his left foot, he shifted it away from where it was lying. There was fine dust beneath. He immediately knew this was the grave of a chameleon. He has been told that the female chameleon cannot lay her eggs the way the hen lays hers. She must die first before the eggs can come out. So, when the eggs are due for laying, the male fights with the female until the female is weak. The male would then drag the female to a hole and bury her alive. From the female's dead and decomposed body, the eggs would emerge to be hatched by the dust. After hatching, there was nothing stopping the infant chameleons from coming out of the dust. If an iron was on their way as was the case here, they would perforate the iron and come out.

---

* *A place fabled by the villagers of Kahugo village to be where ghosts held meetings characterized by eerie lamentation.*

'*Allahu Akbar*!' Mallam Nuhu exclaimed. With the chameleon the woman is the victim of mating, he thought. But with the praying mantis, it is the man that is the victim. A female praying mantis chops off the neck of the male during mating. *'Allahu Akbar!'* he exclaimed again and moved on.

Not far from the grave of the chameleon, he saw an anthill and went to bind the forest by it. When he got to the hill, he could see tell-tale signs of potash around it. There was no doubt about it. The potash was scattered around the hill to drive away the ants. It couldn't possibly have been scattered by cattle owners for their cattle to lick. He walked hurriedly away from the anthill. 'These desperate men of foul fortunes might be up and about already.'

The next anthill he saw, there was *bunsuru fegge* grass growing round it. There was no sign that ants were inside the hill. *A'uzubillahi, shedani rajim!'* he cried close to tears. 'Hasau and Bilia, what have I done to you to deserve this vicious hunt? Oh, my thunderbolt! If only I have you with me; nobody will threaten me this way.' While he was still daze with grave misgivings, his eyes lighted on another anthill not too far away. He went to it and was relieved to find none of the ants' purgatives. His mystic eyes well exercised to knowing which anthill houses ants and which one does not, knew that ants were in this hill. Hastily, he conducted his ritual of binding the evil forces of the forest and moved on into the forest a much happier man than he was in Malmala village.

By nightfall, he was nowhere near Wakiluwa village or indeed any other village. In the daytime when he could see all things, the forest was his castle. At night, the forest held little fear for him when he closed his eyes and saw nothing. What he dreaded in the forest at night were formless images he could not divine their character.

This night was a cloudy, moonless and starless night. The path on which Mallam Nuhu walked, he could not see. He could not even see his right hand that moved to and fro as he trudged on. In the daytime when nothing interfered with his vision, the tray on his head needed not the stability of a hand to keep it on his head. But in this pitch darkness in which the only thing discernible to him were the sounds of his footfall, his head needed the assistance of at least one hand to keep the tray from spilling over when he stumbled on an unseen obstacle on his way.

For Mallam Nuhu, the darkness of this night was kinder in one important respect – it blotted out all dark images that usually invest the night with terrors of menacing figures of uncertain character. For a long time, one body, one soul moved on tick tack, tick tack, tick tack, in a curtain of solid darkness. Here and there, the croaking of a frog, the shrieking of an insect, the hooting of an owl or the howling of a hyena introduced variety into this singular monotony.

His feet at home with paths such as the one he trod experienced little difficulty following the bidding of the path. Like a dog would pick up the scent of a wild animal, his feet were picking the bends and dents of the path leading to the destination of their owner.

But even a dog sometimes misses the trail of a scent. That was what happened to Mallam Nuhu. His right leg went down in anticipation of high ground only to sink into a muddy trough. He fought to regain his balance, but it was in vain. He and his tray went down in an unwholesome, awkward fall. The silent forest about celebrated their fall with a booming echo. For a moment, he and his articles were all mixed in the muddy ground. When he was able to roll clear of the mud, many of his articles had been spun into the mud.

'Poverty is using my lips to scrub the surface of the earth!' Mallam Nuhu cried. 'I have become the sponge of the slimy paths. I … am only but a roving ant ... I cannot sleep because some comfort is needed to sleep. I … cannot die because death being a form of sleep, some comfort is needed to die. So, the violently sick man must first recover before he dies ... God, where is your pity? The vultures – the lepers of the air, cannot see it.'

'Time decides all things,' he said after a turbulent silence. The decision he could not make had been made for him. There was no question of his proceeding beyond this point. In various spots of the muddy ground, some of his treasures lay buried. Who, but a mad man would leave his treasures behind and trudge on? Groping in the dark, his hands located a shrub. He tore off the leaves of the shrub and sat down. He drew up his legs and wrapped his hands around his knees. He shut his eyes; not that it made much difference. Swaying back and forth, he dozed off. His head withered on his chest and his hands came off his knees. He fell hack on the grass and enjoyed a short sleep. In his sleep, he dreamed that Tambuwal was being chased by a snake and he came screaming to him for help.

When he snapped out of his sleep, the moon was out shining with no particular brilliance. But the curtain of solid darkness had been peeled off. Formless figures, which hitherto lay buried under the sand-blind darkness, had assumed their undefined individuality. The real terror of the night had come. That form there looked like the figure of a ghost. The dome-like appearance behind resembled an attacking lion. Ah! this rope-like image in front, is it not a snake? A lizard rustled through a shrub behind him, he spun round to face the lion attacking him. The blind courage that stood by him under the curtain of solid darkness was fast deserting him. Under the new circumstances, he wished he had the eyes of a chameleon that could see in two directions at the same time.

Later, he felt if he must not lose his mind to the haunting fear that now possessed him, he must re-invent the darkness. This he did by shutting his eyes. If he could not see in all directions at once, let him not see in any direction at all. But the fear would not go. The various formless images having entered his mind could not be blotted out by closing his eyes. Still, he persisted with an exercise that was like trying to sleep while awake.

Towards dawn, a cold wind swept past him. Mallam Nuhu's heart leapt down in fear. 'The *jaura* wind,' he murmured. 'I am dead and cold; *the jaura* wind has finally caught up with me.' Then he calmed down. He had just remembered the season was not that of the *jaura* wind.

The *jaura* wind was said to be a cold, freezing column of wind that usually made its passage shortly after harvest during the harmattan season. This column of wind was said to be so cold that it froze to death any living thing whether plant or animal on its path of passage. Whenever it passed through an area, it was said to leave dead trees, animals and human beings on its path. It was an angel of death in a Passover that did not discriminate between *Israeli* and *Egyptian* children. It was said to usually move in the night and towards dawn.

The wind is surely an idle fellow, Mallam Nuhu thought when his worst fear was over and he could relate in a casual way with the wind that moved in waves past him. 'Where is it going to now? you ask this wind moving past me and it can't tell you. Because it has no purpose, it has no destination. Unlike the ants, he had always said the wind has no ambition. Smash up an anthill in the evening and the following morning you are sure to find a new one in the place of the one you smashed. What of the wind? We met it without a home and will die leaving it without a home. The wind was not only an idler, he had always suspected it of rascality and waywardness. That was why to his mind, a wayward fellow was called *Dan iska* in Hausa. He had always, also, thought that because of the character of the wind, ants took an early decision to escape its society and bad influence by sealing themselves up in their hills.

But perhaps the wind is better off than the ants for its lack of ambition, he presently thought. Perhaps that is why it had soared so high and the ants have sunk so low. Perhaps the wind is happier than the ants; that is why it does not die. It does not even age. There are times I think life is *wala*. You don't know what to hold. The wind has wasted time, yet time has not wasted the wind. It is the ants that have honoured time with labour that time is wasting with death. 'The wind is the mad truth prospering in indolence,' he said and issued a mirthless laugher. 'Who is well?' Only...'His body shook and his eyes snapped open. A new brilliance was about him. The source of that brilliance appeared to be behind him. He looked back and saw a small bushel of fire flaring in midair.

'*Jatau,*' he muttered excitedly. 'Wealth … wealth … here comes wealth … Hope like a roused peacock spread her tail and waddled forward.

'But … *Jatau* sits on the ground and twinkles. This light hangs in the air and seems to be moving towards me.' The tail of the peacock fell behind it. His joy dissolved into ashes in his mouth. Fear like *taurikiki* mushrooms sprouted up from the ashes of his joy. 'What could be moving towards me? Poor you Mallam Nuhu,' he whispered when eventually the nature of the light moving towards him impressed itself on his mind. 'You have lost much of your nerves and wits. You can't even tell the light from a hunter's headlamp when you see it. Poor you.'

The headlamp of the hunter had picked him up from the rear and the hunter had aimed his gun at him believing him to be an animal. But as he was about pulling the trigger, something about Mallam Nuhu's figure warned him the creature he was about shooting was not a game. He removed his finger from the trigger and moved nearer the creature. The figure of a man began to take shape. But in his mind, it could not possibly be. For what man would be sitting in a thick forest such as the one they were and in such a far-gone night? If it is not a man and it is not an animal, what is it? A spirit? Fear gripped the hunter.

On his part, Mallam Nuhu's survival instinct communicated a smart idea to his brain. Instead of screaming, he gradually turned his head in the direction of the approaching hunter and smiled into his headlamp.

The hunter screamed. The gun in his hand fell down. Mallam Nuhu gradually rose to his feet and took a step towards the hunter with his fingers fanged out like the claws of a beast. The hunter took to his heels screaming and wailing to the loud speakers of the forests.

Mallam Nuhu laughed at himself. 'Who is well?'

'Even the man that scares another is not well.'

He sat down again and waited for daybreak. It was then not long in coming. When full sunlight came, he went about recovering his scattered articles that could be recovered. He was surprised that not a single article was lost; though some of the articles had lost their original shine as a result of their intercourse with mud. Before leaving, he went to where the hunter's gun laid and examined it with his eyes. Again, he laughed. 'Who is well? Even the forest is not well.' Picking up the articles in his tray, he hurried away from the gun and its scary memory.

Chapter Seventeen

Windows to Lore of Yesterday

Friday, August 7th

Unlike the path between Jita and Malmala, the path between Wakiluwa and Babuna village was a relatively straight path. This character of the path was more visible during the dry season after wild bush fires had consumed the forest laying the path bare. Then sojourners on the path with good eye sights could see each other as far as one kilometre away. When the path was that generous in view, it was not too pleasant to travellers who often felt assaulted by the great distance before them. A distant human figure on this path then was a stationary dark spot on the path. Further accessibility to it, communicated a human figure of no particular identity. Approximation to him defined a personality of a given name.

In the rainy season, the path was not that loose in view. Then, tall grasses under the yoke of dew and gravity drooped to cover the small path. Leafy tree branches hung down as if to raise the yoked grasses.

On the morning of 7th August, Mallam Nuhu was on his way from Wakiluwa to Babuna village to sell his wares. The tray containing his wares was on his head while his right hand held a stick of raffia palm. The stick led the way buffing the grasses to shake off the dew that would have clung to him in a shivery embrace. Several times, he had wondered why the grasses were more eager to shed off their yoke on him than on the ground. This inhospitable attitude of the grasses was to him more like a host choosing to spit on a guest than on a member of his household. In retaliation, he resolved to whack them to good behaviour by the agency of the stick. A rude host deserves a rude guest. His rude reception this particular morning had a biting edge because there was heavy dewfall the previous night and also because he was the first person to pass through the path that day.

His stick went on leading him and his legs went on following the stick – his navigational aid. Let the stick, which by the way is a native of the grasses appropriates their cold reception and spends it on the earth beneath. On he moved, his stick going up and coming down on the grasses – ding dong, ding dong, ding dong. Then it struck a dense shock of grasses and a hare jumped up and raced into the bush. A folk story the hare the wisest animal in folklore tricked the hyena, the most foolish and greedy animal in such lore sprang up in his mind.

According to the story, hare and hyena were friends. Hyena had a very beautiful girl friend in a far-away country that he was planning to wed. One day, he asked hare to accompany him to his girl-friend's village. Hare accepted the invitation and started making preparation for the trip. One early morning, they set out with hyena leading the way. They got to the girlfriend's village at the declension of the sun at noon. The girl was at home. She was such a beautiful girl that had hare staring at her, mouth agape. He was shocked that hyena with all his foolishness could win the heart of such a beautiful girl. Three days after they returned to their village, hare went back to the girl alone.

'Hyena told me you are ready to marry him; is that true?' he asked

'Yes,' the girl replied.

'Do you know that he is my horse and I ride him whenever I feel like?' hare asked, a supreme expression of jest taking over his face. 'In fact, on our visit to you the other day, I rode him most of the way until we started drawing too close to your village. Then, he begged me to dismount so that he would appear before you with some dignity,' he concluded issuing a derisive laughter

'Hah hah hah!' the girl articulated her unbelief in a scornful laughter 'You must be stupid to think I will believe a tiny rat like you will ride on my husband hyena the terror of the forest. Hah hah hah!'

'Seeing is believing,' hare said, less confident than before. Though he had not expected the girl to believe his tall story, he had not expected her to be this clear-headed in her unbelief either. He was somewhat staggered. Still, he pressed on with his scam. 'Since you will not believe my words, this time tomorrow be in front of your house and see how I will ride your fiancé past this village on my way to the next village to attend a funeral ceremony.'

The girl hastily agreed since she was sure nothing of the sort would happen. Hare raced back to his village and went straight to hyena's house.

'I am just returning from the forest,' he said after the two had greeted. 'There, I saw a dead cow decaying away. You know I don't eat meat,' he said in grievous regret of this fact. 'So, I could not eat anything. I left the meat lying there in the forest for flies and vultures. I had already gone past your house when I thought as a friend, I should inform you of the feast flies and vultures are having in the forest. You may want to go and have your share of it.'

Hyena was beside himself with joy. 'I have always known you are my best friend,' he said embracing hare. 'Please let's go so that you can show me the place.'

'No, we can't go now,' hare said. 'You can see it is already getting dark and the place is very far. If we start going now, before we come back, it would be towards dawn; and you know night journeys are dangerous. I think, it is better we wait till tomorrow, so that early in the morning, we will set out. Before the sun rises high into the sky, we will be there.'

Hyena reluctantly agreed. Throughout that night, he did not sleep. All he could think of was that before they get to the forest in the morning the vultures and the flies would have finished eating the cow. He particularly feared the vultures who he saw as the gluttons of the air. Shortly after the first cock-crow, he was knocking on hare's door. 'Wake up my good friend,' he said in the voice of one pursued by gluttony 'Have you forgotten we have a long journey today?'

'But morning is still far off,' hare said, turning comfortably on his bed. 'Go back and wait until the second cock-crow.'

Hyena went back grudgingly. After the second cock-crow, he went back to hare's house. But when he knocked on the door, hare asked in a very weak, sick voice. Ye-s, hy-e-na are you the one kno-cking?'

'Yes, my good friend,' hyena said in a voice thick with intemperate appetite. 'I hope you know cocks have long crowed for the second time? Please come out and let's start moving.'

'But I am not feeling fine,' hare said much fainter than before. 'I have this headache that always descend on me unexpectedly. When you first came, I was very hale and hearty. Now, I can hardly lift my head from my pillow,' he said, pretending to be drawing snot after snot. 'I am sorry hyena; I can't walk a far distance feeling this way.'

'I can carry you on my back,' hyena said, thinking only of the meat being messed up by a flock of useless flies and vultures.

'But the place is very far away,' hare said all joy, all triumph. 'Are you sure you can carry me that far?'

'Why not?' hyena said also basking in a victory of his own kind. 'Is my strength still a secret in this village?'

'Well, I can't stop you if you insist,' hare said shrugging his shoulders. 'But don't later blame me.'

Hyena told him not to bother as he lay down for hare to mount.

Hare mounted hiding a small horsewhip. They set out on their long journey having different destinations and missions in mind. Towards noon, they raced past the village of hyena's girlfriend with hare's symbolic horsewhip held at an all-time high.

There stood hyena's girlfriend staring at the most monstrous apparition of her life. 'So, hare was not lying after all when he said my fiancé is his horse,' she wept. 'Well, I will not marry a man that is another's horse. Instead, I will marry the man that rides him,' she said re-entering her house. That was how foolish hyena lost his girl to crafty hare.

Several times, he had wondered why all folktales that involved hyena always portrayed it as a foolish and greedy animal. Whether it was the hyena with the hare or the hyena with the tiger or some other animal, the hyena always ended up the loser because of its greed and foolishness. Why?

Was the hyena that stupid and greedy? Mallam Nuhu did not think so. He suspected in the ridicule of hyena a veiled anger and hatred of cattle owners whose flock hyena used to devour at night. To vent their anger and hatred against hyena's brigandage, folklore spun round it painting it as a greedy and foolish animal. He suspected herdsmen to be the originators of this folklore. He moved on. He was happy. He was in the forest away from the snares and spite of women. 'But I can only sell to human beings. Why can't even the monkey do with some *tozali* and *garlic*? Poor me.'

By a thick shrub beside the path, he saw the eggs of a dove. His mind went to a folk story of a pregnant woman who packed the eggs of a dove while it was away for a funeral ceremony. The woman was with her mate who advised her not to pack the eggs, but she refused to heed the advice of her mate and packed the eggs. When the dove came back from the funeral ceremony and did not find her eggs, she went into mourning for her lost eggs. Ffuu …uu …, it flew to the house of the woman who packed her eggs and perched on her roof singing:

> Oh, my eggs, oh my eggs, I went to mourn
> Two women came and stood by my precious eggs
> One of them said let's leave these eggs alone
> The other said she would not leave my eggs alone

This woman is pregnant with her only child
She packed and ate all my precious eggs
If I had known I would have packed all my precious eggs
My precious eggs that were better than other eggs
My precious eggs that would hatch me my precious chicks
My precious chicks that would take care of my old age
By your greed you made me a childless bird
If you don't return my precious eggs
I will take the child in your greedy womb
And make you childless as you want to make me.

The bird went on singing this song until the pregnant woman and her mate threshing millet on the threshing ground of their house heard the song. They stopped threshing to listen to the bird's song of lamentation, reproach and condemnation.

The woman who advised the pregnant woman against taking the eggs gave the pregnant woman a meaningful look that said, 'I warned you; now what are you going to do?'

The threat to the pregnant woman's foetus gripped her bowels with mortal fear. After many years of marriage, her foetus was the symbol of her salvation from childlessness to motherhood. A threat to this source of joy was a threat to all meaning in her life. She was horrified beyond articulation of her pleas to the bird. For a long time, she stood listening to the bird without hearing its song of condemnation. Then she went on her knees begging the bird to have pity. She had no child other than the one in her womb; the bird should have mercy. But the bird did not listen to her pleas. It went on singing the same song of damnation. Later, it dawned on the woman that there was not going to be mercy for her by the bird.

She got up and ran behind her room where her guinea fowl had laid some eggs. She packed the eggs and brought them to the bird in restitution; but the bird rejected the eggs.

'What then will I do to save my child since I have eaten your eggs?' she cried beseeching the dove.

'Follow me into the bush,' the dove said. 'I will take you to the eggs of another dove. Pack her eggs and take them to my nest; only then will I forgive you.'

The woman, her body shaking in desperation, followed the dove into the bush. The dove took her to the eggs of another dove and she packed the eggs to the nest of the aggrieved dove. With a sly smile, the dove that received restitution asked her to go home; it has forgiven her.

But as soon as the woman arrived home, the dove whose eggs she had used in restitution, perched on her roof singing the same song of damnation. The woman's heart sank. She started wailing throwing things at the dove on top of her roof. The dove did not leave and none of her missiles hit it. Soon the woman went mad. She ran into the bush wailing and singing the same song of lamentation, which the doves had sung on her rooftop. She died a mad woman in the forest singing the song of her damnation to any dove she came by.

Near river Soka, a jackal leapt across his path. Immediately, a folktale involving jackal, snake, hyena, lion and leopard assumed his mind. So, the story recounted itself in Mallam Nuhu's mind,

One day, lion the king of the forest invited hyena, leopard, snake and jackal to his lair. When all the invited animals were seated, lion who called the meeting informed them of the reason of his convening the meeting. He wanted them to establish a homestead in the forest exclusively for themselves. All the invited animals agreed except jackal. He said he did not want to be part of a homestead of the dead. The others let him be.

Those that approved the proposal sat down to draw up rules that would govern their relationship with one another. The snake spoke first. He said one thing he took serious exception to was for anyone to step on his tail. Anyone that stepped on his tail had by that act shown his contempt for him and he would reply appropriately. After he had spoken, hyena took the floor. He said he might tolerate all provocation, but that of delaying the sharing of meals among members of the commonwealth. He viewed delay in sharing meals an affront on his person and he would not waste time dealing with the offender. After hyena, leopard raised his hand and was permitted to speak. He said he permitted all things save that he did not want to be stared at. Anyone who committed his eyes to his close observation was courting his anger. Lion, the chairman of the meeting spoke last. He said he might tolerate all insolence to his person save that of throwing dust into his eyes. Anyone that did that had amply demonstrated his contempt for him and he would swiftly deal with the offender.

The republic of four for some time enjoyed peace and harmony because each observed his responsibilities to other members of the commonwealth. During this period of tranquility, the snake did not lose his temper, because nobody stepped on his tail. Hyena did not howl in anger because meals were speedily shared. Leopard did not quarrel with anybody because all avoided looking at him beyond normal casual glances. The lion did not roar in anger because everybody took care not to raise dust that might fall into his eyes.

Even with this tranquility it appeared jackal who refused to be part of the commonwealth did not at any time envy the citizens of this small republic. The same cynical statement he made in the first meeting that gave birth to the republic, he continued to make whenever he passed by the homestead of the four animals. 'The country of the dead,' he would say aloud as he walked past the homestead. First, the four animals dismissed his cynicism as the ranting of a disappointed man. Later, they were angered by the persistence of his cynical attitude towards their commonwealth. They conspired to kill him. However, the very day of this conspiracy turned out to be the day the cynicism of jackal was proved to be well founded after all.

That day, after the animals returned from hunting with less meat than they usually brought. The meat was speedily shared among them to satisfy the preference of hyena. Before any animal could go half-way into his meat, hyena had finished eating his and fixed his eyes on leopard who so far had eaten very little of his. Leopard had been offended. He slapped hyena and a big fight started. In the course of the fight, one of the combatants kicked up dust, which fell into the eyes of lion. Lion had been offended. He went into the fight. As the fight degenerated into a mayhem, lion stepped on the tail of snake. Snake had been offended. He too joined the fight. He smote lion who had mortally maul both hyena and leopard. Lion trampled on snake breaking him at various points. Within a short time, all the animals were dead. Soon, jackal walked by. He stopped and surveyed the doomed republic, then remarked, 'the country of the dead.' He laughed and gamboled about as if celebrating the pacification of a truth.

Mallam Nuhu smiled to himself when this story he was recounting in his mind came to an end. He was moving nearer Babuna village. These folklores that had occupied his mind much of the way seemed to have reduced the journey by half. He came by the last stream he would cross to Babuna village. A man was giving water to his camel downstream. Immediately, a folk story involving the camel and hyena came alive in his mind. Camel, so went the story, went into the bush for leisure after he had been offloaded of potash he brought to town. In the bush, he met hyena. Hyena asked him, 'what is your name?'

Camel answered, 'my name is blow-me-with-your-breath-and-I-will-fall.'

Gluttony roared and soared in hyena. 'Do you mean if I blow you with my breath you will fall?' she asked, excitedly.

'Yes, I will fall,' camel said.

Hyena blew her breath at camel and he made a mighty fall. Hyena was happy. Expectations of a big feast whispered to the royalty of her gluttony. She ran home to bring her children and other animals to help her reduce to a feast a clay-footed ogre. She ululated on coming to her homestead. Her children and other animals rushed out to welcome the homecoming of good news.

'Which traitor has fallen this time?' the animals asked together. 'Is it a cow, a sheep, a goat, or that nameless bastard of no rank – a dog?'

'None of your mention,' hyena said, enjoying the edification of attention. 'It is one unbalanced creature that goes by the unbalanced name of, "blow-me-with-your-breath-and-I will-fall." Right now, he is lying in the bush near the village where my breath fell him. He is waiting for us to come and feast as we like. Please, follow me to the great feast.' The other animals fell in step behind hyena.

On the way, a *smart* idea visited hyena and she swiftly communicated it to her co-travellers.

'Let's get *kalgo* ropes and take along with us. When we get where this creature is, you will tie me on him before slaughtering him. The idea is for me to pin him down to make it easy for you to slaughter the hornwort.'

The other animals agreed and a lot of *kalgo* ropes were secured from kalgo trees. When they got to where hyena first met camel, camel was still there but not lying down as hyena had reported to the other animals and had expected.

'No problem,' she murmured to herself. 'What is you name?' she asked camel.

'My name is, blow-me-with-your-breath-and-I-will-fall,' camel answered.

'Phew...u...u....u,' hyena blew her breath against camel.

Down camel went falling on his left side.

The other animals exchanged glances of surprise and excitement. 'Come quick and tie me on him,' hyena said, going to lie on camel. In no

time, she was firmly tied to the back of camel face-
up.

'Now bring the knife and slaughter the
jumbo,' hyena said, panting from the severity of
the *kalgo* ropes around her.

The other animals reached for the knife. But
the moment camel heard the command of hyena
that a knife be brought to slaughter him, he stood
up with hyena on top of him. Hyena shouted
several orders: 'blow him with your breath, blow
him with your breath, quick, quick, quick!'

The other animals blew, but camel refused
to fall. Instead, he started moving towards the
village with hyena on his back. The other animals
ran off into the bush, leaving hyena shouting,
'blow him, blow him down with your breath!'

When camel got to the village, everyone was
shocked to see hyena tied to camel. Children
shouted: 'Yeho! eho! Come and see hyena on top
of a camel. Eho! yeho!'

Camel did not stop anywhere until he got to
the butchery his owner, the chief butcher of the
village, was attending to his meat and customers.
Children's shouts of *yeho* and their missiles aimed
at hyena trailed camel to the butchery. Camel lay
down by his owner's stall. It was then hyena
received the beating of her life from children and
adults. But the owner of camel – the chief butcher,
cut short her ordeal when he added a knife to the
canes used in whipping hyena. The knife neatly cut
the *kalgo* ropes and hyena dived to safety.

However, she did not flee empty mouthed. She pounced on the leg of a cow on the chief butcher's table and ran off with it. 'Block here, hit there!' hyena managed to escape with the cow leg. She got to her cave panting and bleeding from various injuries inflicted on her by the villagers. After berating her child for being uncaring cowards that could neither fell the camel nor follow her to the village, she told them they would not have even the smallest chunk of the meat she had snatched from the chief butcher's table. She started frying the meat.

An appetite-whetting aroma soon possessed the cave. Appetitive saliva was welling up in the mouths of hyena's children. Hyena was in the inner part of the cave while her children were in the outer part. Soon a smart idea came to the youngest child of hyena. Unseen and unheard by mother hyena whose whole attention was on the frying meat, he communicated his idea to his siblings who nodded their assent.

'Please mummy, shift a bit so that I can go inside and bring water for you. You look thirsty,' hyena's youngest child said in a beseeching voice.

'Little rascal, go in,' mother hyena said. 'But remember that nothing you do for me now will make me give you this meat.' She shifted to make room for her child to move into the inner recess of the cave beyond her.

No sooner had the child gone to the uttermost part of the cave than a cry came from within saying, 'please chief butcher, don't kill me. I am not the one who snatched the leg of your cow. It was my mother; please don't kill me!'

The moment hyena heard this plaintive cry and its petrifying message, she ran out of the cave spilling excreta all over the place. She did not return to the cave until after three days. Then her children had since finished a great feast. Even after three days, when she returned, she did not enter the cave straight. She paused outside to listen and observe the presence or absence of danger before she moved in. When she was sure of the absence of danger, she moved in and asked the children how they escaped death in the hands of the chief butcher. The youngest child good in deception mourned: 'oh mummy, why did you run and leave us in the hands of that wicked butcher. He nearly killed us. After taking his meat, he thrashed us like sheaves of hungry rice.'

Mother hyena never heard such a tearful voice. 'Served you right,' she said. 'Since you wouldn't be beaten with me in the village, it is only fair you received your beating in the hush.' Everybody savoured a victory of his own kind.

By a big baobab tree beside the path, a vulture flew above Mallam Nuhu's head. 'Chief sinner and chief penitent!' he saluted the vulture. The vulture, according to a popular folklore, was an incorrigible sinner quick to sin and quick to beg for forgiveness. Once upon a time, went the folklore, animals and birds of the forest held a meeting in the forest where it was agreed that eating carrion of whatever creature is a mortal sin against the God of all creation whose throne was in heaven. The vulture was in the meeting and took part in the decision outlawing the eating of carrion. But the vulture was a bush fly that could not stay away from faeces. He went on eating carrion as if no law had been passed prohibiting the act. However, he had a steadfast conscience. Any bit of meat he pecked off a carcass, he looked up to the sky in full penitence to the Most-High sitting in his throne in heaven. Because of his lack of sincere penance, the vulture is the most wretched and miserable of God's creatures.

'Sarkin Noma, *in Sha Allah*, you will share misery with the vulture all the days of your life!' Mallam Nuhu swore, bitterness replacing the shine that has been on his face while these tales replaced each other in his mind.

He came to an open field sheep and goats belonging to various households of Babuna village were grazing secured to pegs driven into the ground by different types of hammers.

These things look like antelopes and young bush pigs yet to start mating, he thought to himself. And really, are they not? He peered at the sheep and goats in different states of stuffing their bellies with lush grasses for the hunger and tedium relieving engagement of cud-chewing at night. As if to tell him they were neither wild creatures nor adolescent virgins of his thinking, a loose he-goat broke into the open field from a nearby thickset and started tormenting the various nanny goats in the field observing no distinction between its mother and the other nanny goats. A tale involving a he-goat and his wife and children on the one hand and hyena on the other hand succeeded the last folktale in his mind.

'Once upon a time,' Mallam Nuhu in full mirth said in his mind, 'he-goat, his wife and children went to graze far in the forest. They were caught by a heavy rain and got lost. They wandered the forest not knowing which direction home lay. They strayed to the home of hyena where they met monkey – hyena's maidservant. Hyena was out hunting.

Monkey said, 'Ah … he-goat! What has brought you and your family to the home of death? Don't you know this is the home of hyena? For your own good, run before hyena returns; and by my knowing, he can this very moment.'

He-goat's heart thumped wildly in fear. His wife and children started crying lamenting their break with fortune that day 'Come let's run,' the wife said to her husband and children. 'Perhaps fortune may yet smile on us by securing us from the jaws of hyena.' The children ran after their fleeing mother, but their father he-goat called them back.

'Wait woman,' he shouted at his wife. 'What do you think you are doing? Do you think you can escape hyena by running away from this place? How far do you think you can run before he catches up with you anyway? The only way of escape I see out of the jam we find ourselves is to brave danger, stare it in the face and by cunning, outwit it. This is what to do,' he whispered some secret into the ears of his wife. The jittery wife nodded. Quickly, he-goat dragged his family into hyena's cave.

Monkey was shocked to silence by this brazen act of suicide. He shrugged his shoulders and waited for the return of his master.

Soon hyena returned carrying a goat he had killed. Monkey ran to welcome him with the good news of another meat at home.

You said it is he-goat and his family?' hyena asked in a happy tone.

'Yes.'

'Madness has surely come upon them in the worse form it incites people to suicide,' hyena said in a voice full of predation. 'Carry this goat while I move ahead to welcome our guests the best way I know how.'

Inside the cave, he-goat had heard and observed the approach of hyena. He told his wife to put in motion his scheme of confronting death outside. The wife caused their children to start crying emitting strange sounds hyena had never heard. He-goat asked his wife in a loud voice why the children were crying.

She answered, in an equally loud voice, 'it is because they are hungry'

'Have they finished eating the meat of the hyena I killed the other day?' he-goat shouted.

'Yes!' his wife shouted back.

'Ah … ah...' he-goat stammered. 'Well, tell them to be a little patient. We are in the house of another hyena. Perhaps he will soon come back to his house. If he does, he will provide us with a meal very soon.'

All these words uttered loudly by he-goat fell distinctly into the ears of hyena and monkey walking behind him. He paused in fear and asked monkey. 'Didn't you say our guests are he-goat and his family?'

'Yes, they are my lord,' monkey answered.
'If they are as you said, who is he-goat to talk of killing a hyena and waiting for me to provide him and his family their next meal.' hyena asked, suspiciously.

'Truly, it is he-goat and his family,' monkey said frantically. 'He is only playing tricks with your ignorance of his identity.'

'But how can he-goat who fears to go into even the nearest bush to his hut pull this kind of trick against me!' hyena asked of no one.
Monkey said nothing.

'Well, let's move on,' hyena said in a fearful voice. 'If it is an animal I can kill, we will have a feast. If it is not, each of us will commit his safety to his feet.'

'As for our suicidal guests being he-goat and his family, I have no doubt,' monkey said.

'Besides, sparing lion the king of the forest, which animal is stronger than you,' he added for good measure.

'Shut up!' hyena shouted at him. 'The animals that are stronger than me in the forest who can count their number? Let's just go and see who these unnerving animals are.' They moved nearer the cave.

Again, he-goat's wife caused their children to issue the same strange cry. Again, he-goat pleaded with them to be a little patient as monkey had promised to trick hyena into their present habitation. If monkey succeeds in betraying hyena into his hands, their hunger would wither the way cotton withers under the onslaught of wind.

Hyena went wild with anger. He seized monkey by the throat and squeezed. 'So, you conspired to deliver me to death?' he screamed, murder cooing seductively to his sense of vengeance. 'Well, too bad for you. You will die before I do,' he said, mauling monkey to pieces. Then he took to his heels spilling excreta all over the place.

He-goat and his wife inside the cave laughed and congratulated each other. They passed the night in that cave and in the morning were able to find their way back home again.'

Mallam Nuhu had arrived Babuna village and so had trade. From a distance, children's shouts of, '*dankoli, dankoli*! *Ga dankoli*!' could be heard.

Mallam Nuhu responded to the siren of their welcome with:

Kayan koli the beauty herbs
Women who love the beauty fairy
Buy themselves *kayan koli* the beauty herbs
And live happier with their happy husbands
Men who love the beauty fairy
Buy their women the beauty herbs
From dankoli who sells the beauty herbs.

Babuna like Baucha village was a big village surrounded by several smaller villages. Whenever Mallam Nuhu visited this village, he spent close to a month in the village hawking his wares to his numerous customers in the village and neighbouring villages. Depending on which quarter of Babuna or some other village he was taking his wares on a given day, he was likely to sleep in that quarter or village. From Babuna and its neighbouring villages, he proceeded to Dondoni village in the northern part of the Darakuwa plateau.

Chapter Eighteen

The Scent of Death

For three years running, Mallam Nuhu had not been to Dondoni village located in the northern part of the Darakuwa plateau. The reason for his absence from the village was that during the affected years, the village was under the scourge of small pox epidemic. All non-natives of the village avoided it for the years the epidemic lasted for fear of getting infected with the disease and taking it to their villages. But when news came to Mallam Nuhu that the epidemic had left the village he extended his trade to the village once more. He got to the village in the evening and so could make only a few sales before nightfall. At nightfall, he headed for the house of Sarkin Pawa where he used to pass the night whenever in the village. On getting to where he knew the house to be, he was surprised to find it reduced to rubbles. For sometimes, he stood wondering what might have happened. Could small pox have claimed all the inhabitants of the house? If it had, could it have also demolished the house? What about the dark spots he could see here and there which suggested the house had been burned down? Could small pox also have done that? 'No,' he said to himself. 'Something more sinister has happened to this house.' He started moving away from the rubbles of the house. Misery had delivered her puppies in the ruins of the house and they were barking at him. He went to the next house and announced his presence at the gate with *assalamu alaikum*.

'*Amin alaikum salaam*,' a female voice answered from within. Later, a boy of about nine years came to the gate from within.

'Is that not where Sarkin Pawa's house used to be?' he asked, pointing at the rubbles.

'Don't you know he had run away from town?' the boy asked in turn.

'Ran away from town?' he asked perplexed. 'For what? The small pox ...? Well, please, call an elderly person inside for me. Perhaps ...'

The boy looked at him rather too thoughtfully for his age; then went back into the house.

Mallam Nuhu at the gate kept looking towards the rubbles of Sarkin Pawa's house. From where he stood, he could still hear the barking of misery and her puppies resonating in the air around him.

Soon, an elderly man came out to meet him. Tall and frail, this man wore his misery on his forehead. He was a man whose yesterday had offended his today and now took care upon occasion that his today did not offend his tomorrow. Part of this care was to spare friendship for those who that indulgence would confer a benefit.

'You are the man asking after Sarkin Pawa and his house?' the man asked squinting at Mallam Nuhu.

'Yes. Is that not where his house used to be?' Mallam Nuhu asked.

'Yes, but neither he nor his family still lives there.'

'That is obvious enough. What happened?'

'Sarkin Pawa ran away from town. He was owing everybody. He couldn't pay any. His creditors went after his neck the way he had been going after the necks of cows. He fled, and in a very irresponsible manner: He left his family behind.'

'That was too bad,' Mallam Nuhu said, 'When did this happen?'

'About a year ago.'

'So where is his family now?'

'Life has been very unkind to that house, my brother,' the man said throwing a sorrowful look at the ruins of Sarkin Pawa's house. 'About eight months ago, Mallam Gajere who Sarkin Pawa was owing three pounds, set Sarkin Pawa's house ablaze after he quarreled with Sarkin Pawa's first wife.'

Mallam Nuhu felt it was not his business, but could not resist asking what caused the quarrel between Sarkin Pawa's wife and whoever Mallam Gajere was.

'Well, as I heard the story,' the man said, a sad gleam taking over his face. From the manner he pronounced *well*, it was clear the story he was about telling was one he had told several times and each time he told it, he told it with a measure of grief. 'Sarkin Pawa's wife had gone to the market to buy meat where Mallam Gajere also sold meat. She bought the meat from a butcher close to Mallam Gajere. Mallam Gajere was not happy and passed a scathing remark that she would be doing her runaway debtor husband more good if she bought her meat from his creditors. The woman was free with her mouth. She told him that only idiots lent money to others and they deserved nobody's pity. Mallam Gajere answered, 'fine, an idiot will soon visit his idiocy on you.'

'In the night of that day, screams from Sarkin Pawa's house woke most of us whose houses were nearby. Sarkin Pawa's house was on fire. When the fire died down, five children and two adults were burned beyond recognition. As for property, all went with the flames. That same night. Sarkin Pawa's second and third wives fled the village with their remaining children. The first wife who lost all her three children in the fire went mad and had since turned the butcher's part of the market where her husband and Mallam Gajere used to sell meat into her permanent residence. Wherever she went in the daytime, she came back there at night to sleep. During her mental frenzies, she hollered the names of Sarkin Pawa and Mallam Gajere. Because of her occupation of that part of the market, the butchers were forced to relocate to another part. This is the story of Sarkin Pawa and his family,' the man said finally.

Mallam Nuhu's blood ran cold as the man told him the pathetic story of the end of a family. 'Who is well?' he said, meditatively.

'Only the one who flees from his creditors is well,' Dangana replied.

'Has Sarkin Pawa heard the calamity that befell his family in his absence?' Mallam Nuhu asked.

'I wouldn't know if he has since he has not returned since he left the village,' the man said. 'By the way, what are you to him?' he asked.

'Well, we are not really related,' Mallam Nuhu said. 'I am merely dankoli that used to pass the night in his house whenever my trade brings me here and I am to spend the night in the village.'

'Ah! Are you Mallam Nuhu he once told me about?' he asked peering at him again.

'I am he,' Mallam Nuhu said.

'Please enter and sit down inside the vestibule,' the man said. 'You are welcome to my house any day. My name is Dangana.'

'Thank you,' Mallam Nuhu said, but did not move. He was still thinking of the calamity that had befallen Sarkin Pawa and his family. His eyes grew misty with tears. 'Life!' he thought aloud.

'It is an unforgiving money lender,' the man said. 'Please come in.'

It is sad ...'

'Only hyenas are happy in it.

'It is a fraud ...'
'Only the crafty know how to handle it.'
'It makes me wonder ...'
'The depth of its tragedy; please come in.'
'The troubles of life ...'
'One is asleep and the other is awake.'
'It is strange ...'
And we the strangers do not understand it; please sit down.'

Mallam Nuhu sat down on a mat in the vestibule and continued his sorrowful remarks.

'Life...' he murmured.
'It is a trade in opposites,' Dangana said.
'Sadness is the kinsman of happiness ...'
'As happiness is the kinsman of sadness.'
'One man's headache ...'
'Is another man's laughter.'
'When a man is born ...'
'He cries while others laugh.'
'He cries because life is a succession to trouble ...'
'Others laugh because a successor to their trouble has come.'
'When a man dies ...'
'Others cry because a bearer of trouble has betrayed them to more trouble.'
'If life is truly a trade in opposites ...'
'A dead man should be laughing for betraying trouble to fosterage as it betrayed him to toil.'
'Sadness will always escort happiness ...'

'As happiness will always escort sadness.'

'It is an even sadism.'

For a long time, the two men sat in silence, each lost in his own thoughts. Then Mallam Nuhu picked up the thread of their commentary again. 'Sarkin Pawa... Ah Sarkin Pawa.'

'Sarkin Pawa has sold his soul to the wind of his flight.'

'He has become the kinsman of dust devil of the forest spirits.'

'He now rushes past us without a familiar whizz.'

Oh Sarkin Pawa, Sarkin Pawa where are you?'

'Whoever is looking for the vulture in the market, but has not gone to the meat sellers' stalls cannot be serious. Sarkin Pawa is in the plains of the fugitive winds ...'

'The fugitive winds that wander to no destination.'

'Sarkin Pawa, for you there can be no home.'

'For that matter, the wind has always been a refugee.'

A meal of *tuwon dawa* came. Mallam Nuhu ate, his mind never far from the tragedy that played out in the house of Sarkin Pawa. Not that Sarkin Pawa had been spectacularly hospitable to him. But he was not a man to forget favours done to him, no matter how little. Three times he had slept in Sarkin Pawa's house and this was something.

Though on two of these occasions, he was not given any food, the mat he slept and the roof that hung over his head throughout the night were things he held in favour of Sarkin Pawa. The abscondment of Sarkin Pawa again brought to his mind several cases of other butchers who at different times had to flee their towns on account of their bankruptcy. He wouldn't know for sure, but felt a curse must be on a vocation whose practitioners had no record of solvency, least prosperity. This curse if it exists, he felt must be from herdsmen whose wealth constitutes butchers' stock-in-trade. But for a curse, why should a particular vocation suffer the distinction of ruinous indebtedness? Was it Gadau, Gambo, Hashim, Bello, Tanko, Na Ayuba, or Nakawu? All these men, butchers in different villages had at different points in time fled their villages. Some with their families; others, like Sarkin Pawa, alone: all to escape the wrath of their creditors.

'There is no scent in any shit...,' he said in a solemn voice.

'Each is smelling its own smell.'

'Life is a fishing festival ...'

'Every man that catches a fish puts it inside his gourd.'

'Who does not desire ...'

'That in his room there are eggs of an ostrich.'

'Child, love your vulture ...'

'The white-billed stork is only a visitor.'

'What is it?' Mallam Nuhu murmured and yawned without covering his mouth with his hand.

'May the devil not urinate into your mouth,' Dangana said

'May he develop boils on his buttocks if he dares do that,' Mallam Nuhu replied, absentmindedly.

When the two men grew sleepy, Dangana showed Mallam Nuhu an earthen bed covered with raffia mats and a woolen blanket as his bed for the night. The two men bade each other good night. Mallam Nuhu lay down still thinking of Sarkin Pawa and the uncertain curse that hung over butchers when sheep stole him away.

Outside, the skies were growing darker and stormy. A heavy rain was in the air. It started pouring sometime after midnight and went on pouring till dawn. About three hours into the rain, a room in Dangana's house collapsed. Luckily, it was not inhabited by anybody. Towards dawn, another room in which one of Dangana's wives was living collapsed on her and her children sleeping in the room. Two children and the mother were able to escape death. But two other children lay buried in the debris of the collapsed building. A siren of lamentation rent the air. It was what saved Mallam Nuhu. As he raced out to know what was amiss, the vestibule he was sleeping crumbled on his heels. The articles of his trade, however, lay buried under the ruins of the vestibule. At last, he had *sold* all his articles in a single trip. The heavens sighed in a dull lightning that did not merit a thunder; then an uproar of lamentation seized the entire village. The rain had struck in more than one house.

'The snake of the sky is abroad grazing in the clouds,' Mallam Nuhu said, pointing at what looked like a rainbow in the eastern skies.

'He is the hand of the evil one in the air,' someone said mournfully. 'When he falls on a man who will find him?'

The rainbow was seen in Dondoni village and other surrounding villages of the Darakuwa Plateau as a potent natural force with evil and good influences. As an evil force, it was the snake Tiyimba that came out to graze or seek water in the clouds. If it fell on any one, it devoured him at once. But if anyone could find the spot where either end of the rainbow touched the earth, his fortune was made. If a man came across it, he must run in the direction of the sun, for then it could not see him. If he ran away from the sun, it would catch him and he would be totally lost. The rainbow was also seen as a disease which if it rested on a man, he would be done for.

'May the hand of the evil one fall on Tambuwal,' Mallam Nuhu prayed in his heart.

'Oh, evil one we seek refuge from you in the sun,' somebody said.

'But his tongue has already eaten into our intestines,' another man replied.

Chapter Nineteen

Sighs and Tears

Sunday, August 31st

Mallam Nuhu left Dondoni village in despair after losing his wares to the rain that fell in that village. He has been in the trade of *koli* for a long time now and was agitated he was still far from what he wanted to achieve for himself in the trade.

For two days, he roamed the forest between Dondoni and Katula village heartbroken and weak from hunger and distress. He was lost, but was happy he was lost in the forest; not in a town. Over the years he had been in the *koli* trade, he had come to understand and master the forest than he had understood the villages he traded in. He had been able to tame the wildest forest with the mystic powers of anthills, but had failed to tame the most civil village with his patience and civil manners.

The forest he was lost was a vast one. Even for a man that knew it, it was easy to get lost in this forest if care was not taken to note where one had moved from and where he had moved to. All the trees in the forest looked alike and it was very easy to mistake one for the other. Without much thought of where he was going, he had left the path he was walking and went into the forest to hunt for fruits and any wild animal he might be lucky to kill. As he wandered farther into the forest, he soon discovered he had lost direction of the path he had left.

But he did not experience much worry on realising he was lost. So instead of looking for the path, he continued hunting for fruits and animals. It was not him who was lost but the path. If the path loses itself, it would find itself again.

Hunting for fruits and animals, he found little fruits to pluck and no animal to kill. What was his friend the forest telling him? he wondered. Towards nightfall, he found some wild fruits and ate them. At night, he climbed a tree and slept. On the second day when hunger began tormenting him, he went looking for a path that would take him to a village he could find food. While looking for a path, he found a flint. He abandoned searching for the path and went hunting for animals again. He was lucky to kill a bandicoot rat with the big stick he navigated the forest with. Using the flint, he kindled a fire and roasted the bandicoot rat. He carried the roasted meat to a nearby stream. Though he was thirsty, he avoided drinking water until he had eaten much of the meat. To do otherwise would be risking severe stomach pain.

After he had eaten almost half of the bandicoot rat, he cut a big leaf and wove it into a cup. He extended the cup into the stream to take water to drink, but stopped halfway when he observed a little stir in the water. Immediately he knew a chameleon was somewhere drinking water where he wanted to. He withdrew his hand from the stream and looked up into a network of tree branches and leaves that hovered above the stream. It was there the chameleon drinking the water would be; not on the ground with him. From what he knew of the eating and drinking habit of the chameleon, it would sit on a tree and used its thread-like tongue to snap at a fly perching on a shrub below. Sitting on the same tree, it would let down its tongue to draw water from a stream below to its mouth. When people talked of the long necks of the giraffe and the camel that enabled them feed on distant meals and drink distant water, Mallam Nuhu used to wonder why the chameleon whose tongue was longer than the neck of any giraffe or camel was not mentioned.

Much as he strained his eyes and neck looking for the chameleon, he could not see it in the dense foliage above. It had melted into the leaves and was not to be seen. He took the remaining meat with him and went to drink the water upstream.

How funny life is, he thought on his way upstream. If it were a badger he saw drinking the water, he would have hidden somewhere and waited for it to finish drinking for him to go and drink from the same spot the badger drank. The badger was believed to release medicinal properties into water when drinking water in a stream or some other water body. Hunters who knew this, used to hide somewhere to allow the badger to finish drinking water and leave before they would go and drink from the same spot the badger drank. If they did not hide and the badger saw them, it was believed it would release poison into the water instead of medicinal properties. Anyone who drank the water thereafter, instead of being cured of his ailments, would be poisoned.

'A fish that cannot hear the river, will die in the morning of its birth,' Mallam Nuhu said, squatting down to drink water where he elected to. After drinking the water, he carried what was left of the meat to a nearby tree to rest for a while. He had barely rested his head properly on a surface root of the tree when sleep, the mistress of weariness, threw her lullaby over him. He slept quietly for two hours, then started dreaming and talking in his sleep.

'A wonderful life! This is what I have always wanted to prove that labour pays,' the words drooled out of Mallam Nuhu together with the loud snores coming from his open mouth. 'All these horses, donkeys and sheep for me? Wonderful! Who said labour does not pay? He ... e ... e ... e,' he laughed and woke up laughing. It was a bad thing to wake up from a dream laughing. 'If a man laughs in his dream, something to make him cry will soon happen,' he mumbled on waking up. 'God, this is terrible!' he said staring vacantly into the dreariness of his solitary surroundings. For a moment that stretched into a while, his eyes were fixed on the tree he had slept under. Like a slow crawling reptile, his eyes flicked up and down the tree from the roots that provided the pillow he slept on to the dense foliage provided by an intersection of branches of other trees with those of the one he was under. His bewilderment increased with his raking of the tree, and a breathing cloud of mist hung over his vision like the terror of Nabuka[*] 'Jiba, how do I deserve this?' he finally muttered. 'A baobab tree again? Jiba, the wind is spreading its evil seeds fast beyond the sparse throwing of your shadow. It has sown its seeds everywhere in the forest. And the eyes of the moth beetle are fumigating it with their mucus to blind us your children. Ah … I can see madness skipping in the wind towards me. Ah … Sidi. How do I deserve this teasing?' he yawned, stood up and stretched his body full length; then began walking aimlessly about the forest.

'God, how do I deserve this taunting?' he kept repeating the distressing refrain as he roamed the forest. 'Hmm ... Who is well? Does it matter what a man does? What is right? What is wrong? Sarkin Pawa who could not pay his debt ran away from home leaving death behind for his family. Tambuwal who dispossessed me of my rain stone and killed Makama because of it, is sleeping in his

---

[*] *In Darakuwa mythology Nabuka was a giant grey beast that occasionally wondered about in the sliding clouds of the Darakuwa Plateau to the fright of perceiving inhabitants of the plateau*

house laughing at me and mocking at Makama's ghost. Dangana, a man with a good heart, has lost his children to the heavy hand of heaven. I, who has struggled all my life hoping that fortune will one day smile on me, am now being mocked by heaven for losing my wares to the snake Tiyimba and losing myself in the forest. Who is well? Only the mad truth is well… Does it matter? I have lost my wares and I am now lost myself. What is it? Damn the forest. Damn the forest for mocking me!'

He continued wandering in the forest until he sighted an anthill close to the bank of a small river. From the distance he saw it, he thought he could see red patches all over the anthill evidence the water of *fidda firutsa* tree has been sprinkled on it. He moved on without the fear he would have suffered on previous occasions on beholding such a sight. The next anthill he saw, he ran to it and smashed it with his right foot. 'You are foolish,' he said to the ants scattered with the pieces of their smashed habitation. 'Your labours are foolish labours!' he cried, looking wildly around him. 'Yes, you don't beg; so what? The bat that sleeps all day in his nest also does not beg. See why you are so foolish?'

For a long while, he lapsed into silence then sharply launched another tirade; this time with a flurry of activity. 'Let me see the treasures you have been labouring all these years to store for yourselves and your miserable offspring.' He began scooping out the moist soil of the anthill while staring contemptuously at the ants scattered about him. 'These? Ha! ha! ha! These pieces of mess? How stupid you are! Oh; you have no beds to sheep on at night; not even stools on which to rest? Fine. You know what I think? You deserve to die standing and be buried in a lake of fire. Ah Mallam Nuhu you were foolish to go after the manners of these wretched creatures. These … God where is your mercy?' he wailed into the empty bowels of the vast forest.

After sitting by the ruins of the anthill for a long time, he stood up and continued wandering the forest. He was a man in deep thought. He was a body propelled to move by the desire of activity than the desire to reach a destination. His thoughts were walking him into a particular attitude than to a particular place. Slowly, he stopped walking and whispered, '*a,uzubillahi*. What have I done to myself? Mallam Nuhu you are finished! You were yet not finished when you lost your wares; but you are finished the moment you poked your little finger into the face of the forces that gave you security and courage. God, is it a thing for which you can have mercy?' For a long while he stood still his eyes fixed on a distant object an onlooker would have been unable to say what it was. '…But what is it?' he soon blurted out again railing at remorse pricking him with the arrogance of a reproving agent. 'For years I have knocked on their door with my bare feet and they have refused to open up and give me the fortune I seek … Why shouldn't I smash the damn thing with the same feet and damn the consequences? Who knocks these days anyway? Isn't it all a smash and grab thing?' he cried aloud, sending a guinea fowl roosting nearby flying up a fan palm. 'Guinea fowl, it will be well with your bald head,' he saluted the guinea fowl sitting on the branch of the tree. 'Fan palm!' he hailed the tree; 'your shade is not for those near you, but those far from you. Guinea fowl, you can see why you are on the wrong tree and why I will prevail over you?' His eyes flitted in the direction the guinea fowl had flown from looking for a stone but instead fell on a heap of eggs in a big nest. He forgot about the stone and moved closer to the eggs. He counted them.   There   were   forty-one   eggs.

'Wonderful,' he said. 'How could one guinea fowl lay all these eggs?' He looked up at the guinea fowl perched on the tree branch and found it staring intently at him. He thought he could see a plea in the eyes of the guinea fowl that he should spare its eggs. For a moment, he was overtaken by sympathy for the guinea fowl, but quickly checked the feeling. 'Man, this is not a sentimental world,' he scolded himself. 'This is a hard, wicked world without room for sympathy. Dangana is a man of sympathy, where has it taken him? These eggs are part of a restoration from *Allah Tabarka Wata'ala.*' He removed his cap and packed the eggs into it. 'But you are lost Mallam

Nuhu; what restoration can you have with the hyena behind you and the snake in front of you? Ah ...'

The guinea fowl on the tree started clucking wildly jumping from branch to branch. At first, he ignored it. But when its clucking grew fiercer, he went looking for a stone again, but found none. 'Who has packed the many stones in this forest?' he fumed. Is something fighting for the guinea fowl?' His mind faltered and his body became tensed. But he soon shook his head and went on searching for a stone. In the end, he could only find a piece of wood. He swung the wood at the guinea fowl with a curse. The guinea fowl jumped to a branch slightly higher than the one it was before and clucked even louder. He hissed and started walking away. The guinea fowl followed him jumping from tree to tree. Suddenly he stopped walking, paralysed by a numbing fear. 'What am I walking myself into with my eyes wide open?' he asked himself. The story of the dove with the greedy woman had just seized his mind. For a long while, he remained standing, his mind darting about for an escape route. Then he laughed, pointing at the guinea fowl. 'Guinea fowl, the dove had a better case than you,' he said. 'It went for a funeral ceremony – a compassionate thing to do, and came back to find its eggs stolen. You, guinea fowl have been idling around at home while other well-meaning guinea fowls are at funeral ceremonies. I have not stolen your eggs.

You were looking at me when I was packing them. Your eggs? I doubt if a wayward guinea fowl like you could have laid all these eggs. You must have stolen them from a guinea fowl that has gone for a funeral ceremony. Ha! ha! What? As you can see, I am not pregnant. Which pregnancy of mine will you threaten?'

'You have a son.'

'You can't take my son.'

'Yes, I can.'

'La ilaha ilahuwa,' Mallam Nuhu cried in fear. 'No, no, you can have your eggs back.' He started walking back to where he packed the eggs. When he got to the nest, he put back the eggs as near the position he first met them as possible. When he had finished putting back the eggs, he went back to the smashed anthill. He knelt down by the ruins of the hill and prayed, 'God, some jinn entered me while I was asleep in this forest. These jinn are dancing in my head ... God, what is it? There is madness in the ... wind. Let those who understand the language of the wind listen. Please somebody should say something Ah ...'

While still kneeling down by the ruins of the anthill, his eyes fell on a small tiny path half covered by grasses. His spirit soared. He was surprised he had not noticed the path before. He got up and moved to the path to look at it closely. His knowing eyes told him it was a path that leads to a village. He picked the path and started walking towards the next village and after that the next – a

dispossessed man whose life had become a joke he
could not laugh at.

Chapter Twenty

The Past Appeared with a Kind Face

Saturday, September 6th

Mallam Nuhu got to Kyali, one of the many villages he could not say how many times he had gone through in the course of his trade, to find a big ceremony going on. He moved closer to see what the gathering was about. From where he stood on the fringes of the crowd, he had an uninterrupted view of a fat man who was being applauded by a flock of praise-singers. The praise epithets came in torrents, some bordering on the blasphemous: *Tajiri mai ruwan sha. Takawar ka lafiya masun abu? Sunkuye, masgaye gyara dai Zaki. Dangaladima mai takalmin karfe, kowa ka taka, ya taku. Sarkin Gwagwala, a hauka azame ka hau mutum ka zauna daidai. Shehu jikan shehu, kowa ya rantse da sunnan ka ya tsira.*

The man was gloating over the various praise names nodding his head and giving the *Gamji* salute to the praise-singers as a symbol of royal approval of their praises. Beside this man of visible affluence and royalty sat another man. This other man was a different sort of man from the merchant of the praise-singers. Except that his clothes were a shade cleaner, they were not more expensive than those Mallam Nuhu was wearing.

And except that his body was cleaner and fresher, he was not fatter than Mallam Nuhu.

Sitting beside the baron of the praise-singers, this other man in the eyes of Mallam Nuhu looked like a bronze earring beside a golden necklace. By his severe bearing towards the praise-singers, the austere man seemed ill at ease with their avalanche of praises. From the frequent conversation between him and the merchant of the praise-singers, Mallam Nuhu concluded the two must be friends or at least close acquaintances. However, he wondered how two people of apparent different social classes could be such friends or acquaintances. He tapped the shoulder of a man standing near him and asked what the ceremony was about.

The man he tapped looked like one who life had dispossessed. But he also looked like one who had the spirit to wrest that which was his due from the tyranny of his situation. 'It is a wedding *walima,' he told* Mallam Nuhu.

'Who is the groom?'

'The man sitting close to the man the praise-singers are praising.'

Mallam Nuhu was surprised. All along he had thought the prince of the praise-singers was the horn of the ceremony. 'Why are the praise-singers not attending to him then?' he asked the man again.

'Because he does not like praise-singers. He gives them no money,' the man said. 'In fact, I think they came to this ceremony because of his friend who is their man.'

'Very little gain for rats in a ceremony they are not wanted,' Mallam Nuhu involuntarily remarked, then fell into a thoughtful silence. The austere man is my soul mate. For I do not like people who live by praise-singing. They are shameless layabouts that have lost their own dignity in the worth of others. I cannot understand why it should be the official engagement of any man to debase himself to praise others. Yes, this man thinks like me; or thinks the way you used to think, a voice from within him said.

'Well, well; there you are not too far from the truth,' he replied the voice, cheerfully. 'What? Well, well the way I used to think indeed. Presently, I think these praise-singers have found the favour of living without shame. They don't seem worse off for listening to the wind and embracing the mad truth. Look at their flesh, look at their clothes. Ah! Sidi, where are you?'

'But the groom does not look like he has much money,' Mallam Nuhu said to his informant after sometime.

'Don't be deceived by his appearance,' the man said. 'There is no one in this gathering that is the equal of that man in money. People call him the shepherd of money. Like a Fulani man who rears cows but seldom eats meat, that man rears money but does not enjoy it.'

'Then he will not know want.'

'That is very true. Today, he has wealth, but is in rags. Tomorrow if his wealth divorces him, he will remain in the rags he is wearing today. No one can laugh at him. His true fortune is in his rags.'

'Fortune comes in rags,' Mallam Nuhu whispered to himself.

'What did you say?'

'No, I was only speaking to myself.'

After sometime, Mallam Nuhu felt he had no reason standing to watch a ceremony that had nothing to do with him. However, after persuading himself to leave, this moment, that moment he would leave and continue with his journey, but he hung on like one charmed to remain where he was.

The flock of praise praise-singers were soon replaced at the centre of the arena by the Master of Ceremonies who had invited *yan bori* to the arena. Mallam Nuhu was still where he was. Indeed, with the coming of the bori dancers his desire to leave pulsated to a dull, sneezing itch.

Bori dance was the dance of the spirits. It was a dance by devotees of the *bori cult*. A person did not become a member of the b*ori cult* unless he was touched by spirits of the mountains. Usually, people got into *bori* when they were sick and had gone to look for a cure from a native doctor who himself was possessed by the spirits of the mountains. The native doctor, on examination of his patient, would come to a decision whether herbal medicine would cure the patient or he would have to be initiated into the *bori cult* because certain spirits he had offended had *touched* him. If the native doctor was of the opinion the patient had been *touched* and it was initiation into *bori* that would cure him, the patient was initiated and the sickness that necessitated the initiation disappeared completely from the body of the patient in full possession of the spirits. Whenever the sickness sought to come back, the call tunes of the spirits possessing the patient was played and the spirits in him were roused into war with the sickness conquering it. The patient would start jumping and falling on his buttocks saying insane, indecent and unintelligible things.

To a non-believer in the *bori* therapy, the cure looked like trying to cure sickness with madness. The patient was made mad and so could no longer feel the pain of his sickness which though was still very much in him. But to devotees of *bori*, it was a perfect cure.

Devotees of *bori* got invited to festivities to entertain the guests with their weird and breath-taking performances. Before *bori cult* members went into the *bori* dance, there must be a musician who could play the *goge* or *garaya* and who knew all the call-tunes of spirits of the mountains. Each spirit had its separate and distinct call-tune. In this dance, the dancer if man, was the horse and if woman was the mare. The spirit was the rider. The spirits were individualistic like humans. Each was supposed to wear a distinct costume. *Dangaladima* wore *saki* wrapper, a cap, a black *saki* gown, a pair of *saki* trousers and white turban. *Sarkin Dutse* wore only a native blanket. These different dresses must be worn whenever the possessed performed the *bori* dance. *Bori* dance was as rigorous as it was weird. Because of the rigour and bodily abuse the dance entailed, there was a popular Hausa saying that, *Ba a bori da sanyi jiki* – Bori dance can't be performed with a lazy body. How the possessed dancer danced was the way the spirit inside him danced. If the spirit was emitting foam from its mouth, the possessed human dancer would emit foam from his mouth. If it was swallowing flames of fire, the dancing human body would be swallowing flames of fire. If it screamed in a frenzy of performance, the human body would stream in a wild orgy of performance. Even the drummers for the dance were possessed drummers. Their drumbeats had that eerie edge that pertained only spirits.

Good Moslems were supposed to consider the *bori* dance devilish and unworthy of their patronage. Yet, of all the cultural displays in the wedding *walima*, none commanded the attention of the wedding guests like the *bori* dance. A roaring excitement ripped through the crowd as the dancers acted their awe-inspiring ancient celebration of the spirits supernatural feats among men.

After a considerable time of the *bori* dancers' performance at the centre of the wedding arena, a man to the right of Mallam Nuhu who since the *bori* dance started had not been able to take his eyes off the dancers for a moment even when an insect was biting him behind his ear, in a trance said, 'but why did he invite them?' It was not clear whether he was speaking to the man beside him or to himself; but given his hypnotic-like state, the latter seemed more probable.

Whichever was the case, the man beside him heard him and asked in return, 'why have you been watching them with the eyes of a man looking for something inside a chicken pen?'

'Rascal that you are,' the first man said

'Oho.'

'My only concern is that by inviting them, he has made himself a kinsman of the devil. He has soiled his name and that of his family for life.'

'What about you that can't take your eyes off what he has brought?'

'I am only watching.'

'He only invited them for you to watch.'

'Rascal that you are.'

'In the day, we all put up faces of disgust at the sight of the mad woman ...'

'But at night, some of us follow her into her dirty shack to make love to her ...'

'Some with the hope of becoming rich.'

'Some for the fun of it.'

'Oho.'

The *yan bori* were in the peak of their performance when the man said to be the groom stood up and started spraying money on each dancer. What remained of the bundle of money, he tossed into the air. The drumming of the spirits took a feral turn. As he was about to turn and head back for his seat, his eyes fell on Mallam Nuhu. For a moment, he stood in a dwam trying to recall where he knew the face. Recollection soon came. He smiled at Mallam Nuhu while beckoning him with his hand to come.

Mallam Nuhu was confused. He was not sure the beckon was addressed to him. He thumped his chest with his index finger – a loud way of asking, 'is it me?' Many people standing in front of him also thumped their chests. The man shook his head against them and said, 'the man standing on a ridge behind and wearing a white long cap. It was a clear address to Mallam Nuhu; still he thumped his chest again to confirm his invitation.

'Yes, you,' the man said and started moving to his seat. Mallam Nuhu followed him in suspense.

The man sat down and indicated an empty seat by his left to Mallam Nuhu. He sat down wondering what the man's gesture of friendship was all about. The Bori dancers finished their performance and filed out. The Master of Ceremonies took the floor again and was in the process of saying something when the groom beckoned him to come. He whispered something into the ear of the Master of Ceremonies who soon announced to the gathering that the groom had something important to say.

Mallam Nuhu's suspense deepened.

The groom stood up and thanked the gathering for making time to be at his wedding *walima*. From the way he spoke, it appeared it was not the first time he was thanking his guests in the course of the ceremony.

'The main reason of my addressing you this moment is to introduce to you a man I am indebted to in two important respects,' he said in an emotional voice.

A hush of curiosity fell on the crowd.

The groom turned to Mallam Nuhu and said, 'Baba, please stand up and come here.'

Mallam Nuhu's heart spun an emotive cyclone. He stood up and walked to the groom.

'This man standing before you, I am heavily indebted to in two important respects,' the man repeated in a passionate tone.

A din of regard rose from the crowd and settled on Mallam Nuhu.

'This man standing before you showed me love when I was a child in this village running around half-naked like many of my age mates,' the groom continued. 'One afternoon he was in this village for his trade as usual. I was running past him on the path that leads to our house when he called me and gave me *kulikuli* he was eating. Standing here before you, I can still remember the size of the *kulikuli* he gave me and how tasty it was. It is as if it was yesterday this thing happened.'

The crowd amazed by the groom's vivid recollection of a minor episode in the distant past broke into small conversing groups, most people shaking and nodding their heads in amazement. On his part, Mallam Nuhu was shocked by this revelation. Under no stretch of memory could he recall the incidence that was so firmly etched on the memory of the groom.

My second important debt to this man is that to him I owe my inspiration to go into business and also to him I owe my perseverance in it,' the man continued. 'When I was a child in this village, and well into my adolescence, I watched with respect and admiration the commitment of this man to his trade. Day and night, rainy season and dry season, cold and hot season, this man moved from village to village, hawking his wares to people in need of them.'

Someone among the flock of praise-singers hissed, apparently unimpressed by Mallam Nuhu's profile of industry. Another whispered, 'a dog looking for a name has been called Bello.'

'And after all this effort what have I to show for it?' Mallam Nuhu thought despairingly. 'Well, well.'

The groom threw a contemptuous look in the direction of the praise-singers and continued. 'I felt and still feel that if a man commits himself to any honourable vocation with the same zeal and determination I saw in this man, *Allah Subuhana Wata'ala* who is not an oppressor, will definitely reward him with wealth one day. So, I went into cotton business and Allah has blessed my hard work in that business. As you all know, because of this man I became rich, is better than because of this man I became poor,' he added with a sagely bearing. To Mallam Nuhu, he said, 'that little boy, you gave *kulikuli* to so many years ago; that little boy, you inspired into business a long time ago, is now a multimillionaire and is here to wipe your tears.'

Outside the flock of praise-singers, people clapped. Shouts of *Allahu Akbar*! rent the air. The flock of praise-singers among themselves whispered boo and hoo, chill and shoo.

'I am not a stomach that forgets the generosity of yesterday,' the groom went on. 'You will sleep in my house today and tomorrow I will show my little gratitude to you. Then, don't thank me but Allah that is not an oppressor of anybody. A man that opened his door to make gifts to people yesterday will open his door today or tomorrow to receive gifts from people.'

'When such a man falls into a crevice ...' someone said.

'He will find a ladder on the wall of his falling,' other people finished off for him.

'What lies before a man ...'

'Is more than what lies behind him.'

Mallam Nuhu and the groom walked back to their seats and sat down after the groom's speech of appreciation. The marriage walima continued, but Mallam Nuhu could only follow it with scant attention. His mind was alive with prospects of an uncertain character.

When the ceremony ran its full course, the groom who later gave his name as Abdullahi took Mallam Nuhu to his house where he was given a reception fit only for royalty. The following day, the man gave him a box full of new pound notes and asked his driver to drive him as near his village as a motorable road would take them.

Chapter Twenty-One

A Happy Return

Sunday, September 7th

'Time decides all things,' Mallam Nuhu said as he was chauffeur-driven home with a lot of treasure that promised a new beginning for the village tradesman. 'Man is good, man is bad; what can anybody do?' he kept repeating to himself as they drove on.

The road was an untarred road full of potholes. The car was picking the motorable, less bumpy parts of the road the way a hen picks grains of corn from the ground. Even at this slow speed, Mallam Nuhu and the driver were thrown about with other items inside the car like several pieces of coins in a corrugated tin. As they drew near where Mallam Nuhu would have to disembark because the road could not be managed with a car beyond that point, a loud shout of the name Mallam Nuhu reached the two men in the car distinctly. Mallam Nuhu looked back sharply and saw a man in rags running towards them with a black object held high in his hand. The driver of the car viewing in the rear mirror the man from whom the shouting was coming, did not turn, but pulled the car to a stop in the middle of the road. The road unfrequented by vehicles, he did not feel the need to pull off it.

Mallam Nuhu whose eyes were fixed on the man like intent bugs, soon discerned Tambuwal and his thunderbolt held in Tambuwal's right hand from the theatrics of waving hands, a swinging head, and clouds of spurting dust. He opened the car and got out as the apparently mad man drew nearer them. He stood behind a tree beside the road and peered at Tambuwal. The driver remained seated in the car unmoved by what was going on about him.

'Mallam Nuhu, take your cursed rain stone!' Tambuwal cried hurling the thunderbolt at Mallam Nuhu. Foam was coming from every part of his mouth. The foam mixed with his sweat formed an unsightly slob by the base of his neck.

Mallam Nuhu jerked his peering face behind the tree to avoid being hit by the flying rain stone. The thunderbolt hit the tree he was standing behind and rolled to the ground.

'Instead of fertilising my farms your cursed stone has been killing my crops,' he mourned. All of a sudden, he laughed and danced about the road in a swing-swang.

Speechless and numb with shock, Mallam Nuhu and the driver watched Tambuwal danced on the road foaming in his mouth and pissing in his trousers. After, he was tired of dancing, he ran into the forest shouting, 'yes, I killed Makama. The idiot deserved to die. Who told him the world is a place you tell the truth! Who told him the world is a place you keep faith!'

Mallam Nuhu picked the thunderbolt from where it laid on the ground and re-entered the car.

'Who is he?' the driver asked.

'It is a long story,' Mallam Nuhu replied.

Without further inquiry and explanation, the car began to move once more. The driver discharged Mallam Nuhu and his treasure by the bank of River Nadewa, which had no motorable bridge over it. The two men bade each other farewell and parted. Mallam Nuhu continued his journey his mind possessed by the last words of his benefactor as he was leaving the man's house, and his recent encounter with Tambuwal. With deep regard and affection, the man had said, 'Baba dankoli, you have become the ground fortune must fall on. You are everywhere and fortune cannot avoid you.'

'What a paradox,' he said quietly to himself, then laughed. It was the sort of laughter he celebrated the flight of the hunter in the forest. 'Are there such things as sanity and madness in this fairy world?' he continued, musing over the man's statement. 'Here am I, a man that has all his life spurn the mad truth ending up as the mad truth myself. Here am I, a man whose every action to denounce the mad truth has planted the mad truth in him. Here is Sarkin Noma who when sane had no conscience, but now tells the truth in madness. Certainly, all the blight of this world comes from sanity. There would have been more good in the world if there were fewer sane men. The world indeed is a strange place and we the strangers will never understand it. Perhaps, it is a mad world too; a mad world no one can lay claim to sanity. Perhaps!

As he made the turn that placed his house before him, he saw his wife in her veil leaning out of their vestibule and bidding farewell to a young man he did not know. His face darkened with misgivings. 'Man is bad, man is good; what can anybody do? What is this strange young man doing in my house in my absence?'

On seeing him, the young man shouted, 'Iya, here he comes!'

Mallam Nuhu's wife ran out of the vestibule holding something wrapped in white cloth toned brown by use and age. She fell beside Mallam Nuhu a couple of yards in front of the vestibule crying 'Maigida, the king without a palace you have been serving in the fields has arrived home ahead of you. The god without a shrine whose providence you have been chasing in the desert has set up camp in your house. The homeless maid you have been courting in the wilderness has finally accepted you as her husband. This is money sent to you by Alhaji Shekarau *tajirin* Landa.'

'Yes, Alhaji gave me this money to bring to you,' the young man said. 'He said the *kanhu* you sold to him two months ago has completely healed the chest pain he had come to believe will be his death'

'Waiting for you inside the house is an *asusu* I have been keeping money I removed from your *asusu* to make you save more,' his wife said grinning with a generosity of spirit she had never known.

Mallam Nuhu wept.

A Glossary of Hausa and Arabic Words and Phrases

Allah subuhana wata'ala God the established King
Allah tabarka wata'ala   God the king of all
Allahu Akbar: God is the greatest
Alewa; Sweetmeat
Amin Alaikum salaam wa ramatullah: Amen, may the peace of God be upon you also.
Assalamu alaikum:May the peace of God be upon this house.
AsusuA small earthen or metallic container use for saving money.
Azahar: An Arabic word for Moslem 2 p.m. prayers.
A'uzubillahi: God protect us from the devil.
Ba a bori da sanyin jiki: You can't be involved in bori and be sluggish.
Barka da war haka Agwai: Good day Fulani man.
Barka da yamma: Good evening.
Bazarkwella: Brown Sugar.
Borkono: Pepper.
Bororo: A metaphor for a nomad.
Dadawa: Local maggi made from locust beans.
Dage Na Halima, kyau fada akwana anayi: Badger, husband of Hallima, the beauty of a fight is for it to be all-night long.
Dan iska: Rascal
Dankoli: A hawker of women trinkets.
Dan Galadima Mai Takalmin

karfe; kowa ka taka ya taku: Prince with iron shoes, whoever you march must be bruised
Ga kayankoli: Here are women trinkets for sale.
Garaya: A local guitar
Goge: A local guitar smaller than the garaya.
Iblis: Devil.
Iman: Faith.
Kanbu : A herbal medicine.
Kubewa: Okro.
Kuka: A local soup ingredient.
Kulikuli: Groundnuts dry cake.
La'asar: An Arabic word for Moslem 4 p.m prayers.
Laya: Charm to ward off evil.
Mai-unguwa: Ward head.
Maman: A general nomenclature for a layabout.
Maijin Hajiya: A big for nothing man.
Ranka dade: May you live long.
Saki A male inner wear.
Sarkin gwangwala a hau ka azame ka hau mutum ka zauna daidai: An expression of praise for a
king that suffers no humiliation from anybody rather is the one that subjects others to humiliation.
Samu: A man who overrates his possessions.
Sarkin dutse: Chief of the high lands.
Sarkin noma: Chief of farmers.
Sarkin Pawa: Chief butcher.
Shedani rajim: Secure us from the devil.

Shehu jikan shehu, kowa ya rantse da sunana ka ya tsira: Prince, whoever swears by your name is saved.

Tajiri Mai ruwan sha: Rich man of means.

Takawarka lafiya masu abu; Sunkuye, masgaye gyara dai zaki: An expression of praise that seeks to edify the movement of a rich man.

Tozali: Dark eyebrows and eyelashes powder used mainly by rural women as make-up.

Tuwon dawa: A solid Hausa meal made of ground sorghum and taken with soup.

Wala: A creature with many legs which if one of its legs is caught, it leaves behind that leg and move on making the effort of catching any of its legs futile.

Walima: Marriage feast or indeed any feast.

Yan dabba: A clan of tough men who live by stealing.

Yan tauri;   A clan of crooks who live by stealing and sometime jab themselves with knives without drawing blood to demonstrate toughness.

 Yauwa: Thank you.